A TASTE OF LOVE
M.A. GONZALES

TUSCAN HEAT

Tuscan Heat

Copyright © 2019 by M.A. Gonzales

Copyright © 2019 M.A. Gonzales
First electronic publication: **April 2019**
First paperback publication: **April 2019**
Revised electronic publication: **December 2020**
Revised paperback publication: **December 2020**

M.A. Gonzales

www.magonzales.net

All Rights are Reserved. No part of this book may be used or reproduced in any manner whatsoever without written permission, except in the case of brief quotations embodied in articles and reviews. The unauthorized reproduction of this copyrighted material is illegal. No part of this book may be scanned, uploaded, or distributed via the Internet or any other means, electronic or print, without the author's permission.

NOTE FROM M.A. GONZALES

This book is a work of fiction. The names, characters, places, and incidents are a product of the writer's imagination or have been used fictitiously and are not to be construed as real. Any resemblance to persons, living or dead, actual events, locale, or organizations is entirely coincidental. The author does not have any control over and does not assume any responsibility for third party websites or their content.

Published in the **USA**

Cover art by: R.L Kenderson Cover Designs
Editor: Heather Leigh

TUSCAN HEAT

Dedication

For love
Old and new
Lost and found
And second chances

TUSCAN HEAT

Chapter 1

"Why don't you skip to the part where he began fooling around," Lilian suggested, pulling freshly baked loaves of bread from the old-style cast-iron oven.

Popping a red grape into her mouth, Marlina rolled her eyes and ignored her sister's request. She didn't want to hash out her pathetic marriage. "How did you manage to talk Nonna into putting a new oven in her kitchen?" Nonna was their grandmother, similar to the American *Nana*. Marlina knew Lilian didn't do small talk, but Marlina did—especially when it was a subject she didn't want to discuss. And the last thing she wanted to talk about was Adam and his two-timing ass.

"It wasn't easy, believe me," Lilian muttered, flipping the bread upside down on the wire cooling rack. Picking up her wine glass, she took a large sip of the crisp burgundy wine and handed it to her. "Chug that! Embrace your anger and tell me what happened."

Rolling her eyes, she did as her sister suggested, downing the wine in one large gulp. *Maybe Lil is right; maybe getting it off my chest will make me feel better.* "There isn't much to say—one day we were in love, and the next we weren't. Happens all the time," Marlina shrugged.

"True enough. However, what doesn't happen all the time is a woman's husband running away with a twenty-one-year-old intern from his office."

She winced at the harsh truth in Lilian's words. No, that didn't happen every day, yet it happened to her. "I still can't believe it." Groaning, she reached for the wine bottle and refilled her glass. *If I'm going to relive this, I'm going to need more wine.* "His career at the firm was flourishing, and his classes at the university were always full. He was always so busy all the time. I never thought he had time for an affair."

"Men are never too busy to have an affair, Lina. They always got time for a new piece of ass," Lilian muttered, aggressively chopping some sun-dried tomatoes.

Marlina chose to ignore her sister and her murderous plight on the tomatoes. "He had so much going for him, and he just threw it away on some...some...." saying this part was always so hard.

"Teenager?" Lilian stated plainly, quirking her brow as she began scooping up the chopped tomatoes and tossing them into the wooden salad bowl.

"She's in her early twenties," she corrected.

"That's not saying much. When a forty-year-old man develops a sexual relationship with a woman half his age, and a student no less, it's just...."

"Every man's dream?" Marlina questioned.

"I was gonna say pathetic."

"You know what else is pathetic?" Marlina asked, a sad smile playing upon her lips as she sipped her wine a little more slowly. "Every student who takes his class hangs on his every word. I mean, he is attractive." She shrugged. "Something was bound to happen sooner or later, I guess."

Lilian picked up the wooden spoons and began tossing the salad. "*Delusione,* disappointment will be biting her in the ass soon. You know what they say, a leopard doesn't change its spots."

Smiling, Marlina nodded. "Yeah. Mistresses aren't fun once become wives."

"You couldn't have walked away without doing something, anything." Lilian stopped tossing mid-stroke. "What did you do?" she asked, curious.

"I stuck the water hose in the ground and left the water on before I left. I still had two days there, so I'm pretty sure the foundation was nice and flooded when they got there with her stuff."

Lilian squealed. "You didn't!"

Her shoulders shook with laughter. "I did. I tried to be the bigger person, but who am I kidding?" Marlina chuckled. "That was my house before she decided she wanted it. Couldn't she have just taken the husband and left me the home?"

"It is a beautiful house, a little big for two people. Maybe the water will cause damage or mold or something." Lilian smiled, looking over at her. Immediately, her smile fell as she took in the look on her sister's face. "Lina, what's wrong?"

Closing her eyes briefly, she fought back the bitter taste at the back of her throat. This part always made her sick. "It won't just be the two of them for very long."

"What are you talking about?" Lilian asked in confusion.

"I didn't tell you?" her voice cracked, and she cleared her throat. It wasn't like divorcing Adam left her devastated, that's why she didn't understand why this part hurt so much. "She's pregnant," Marlina whispered. The last thing she wanted was a family with Adam, and he had said the same thing. They were both invested and concentrating on their careers. Turns out, he wasn't as against the idea as he pretended. What hurts the most was knowing that she spent all those years, put up with all the shit he threw at her during the years, and for what? He never saw a future between them. The least he could've done was let her go or, better yet not marry her at all.

"What?" Lilian shrieked. "You've got to be kidding me."

"Nope."

"What the hell is he thinking?" Lilian huffed. "No doubt he's popping a little blue pill to accomplish that shit."

She snorted. "Should have been taking one with me too."

Lilian stared at her wide-eyed. "You wanted kids?"

"With him? Hell no." She couldn't ever imagine having kids with his uptight ass. He was too much like her mother. "The sex just sucked."

"It wasn't ever good?"

Marlina simply shook her head. "Never." Frowning, she reached down and scooped up a hand full of *Crescenza* cheese and spread it across the top of the salad. "Even when we were first dating, there really wasn't any spark or passion. It was so—formal."

Lilian frowned, shaking her head while she set up a platter of *Caprese Salad*, which consisted of fresh mozzarella, tomatoes, basil, and olive oil, along with *Prosciutto*. The simple salad was one of Lilian's favorite dishes. "Formal? We're not rich or royalty. How the hell can a relationship be formal?"

"Mom set it up." Her jaw was sore from the number of times she had clenched it while thinking about how interfering and meddling her mother was. "Mom always had a plan for my life, right down to practicing law." That's right, she was a lawyer, and she hated it.

Vivian, her mother, had pushed her in that direction for as long as she could remember. She wasn't lucky like Lilian, who was a disappointment in their mother's eyes. They'd always bumped heads, and if their mother had wanted Lilian to do something, then she usually did the opposite.

Marlina, on the other hand, was the perfect daughter for their mother. Always doing as she was told, buckling down, studying instead of going to parties or dates like most of her friends, and no matter how hard she tried not to, she always gave in to her mother. She went to NYU, pre-law, and went on to Columbia law school—just like her mother planned. Her whole path, the entire career course, was something she didn't want, but she went along. It was the same with Adam; she never spoke up just always went along with whatever he wanted.

Looking at her sister, she smiled sadly. "I wish I could've been more like you."

"What are you talking about? How did we go from Adam sucking between the sheets, to you wishing you were like me?"

She looked out the casement window to her left, staring at the tall, springy green Cypress trees outside. "You've always been who you wanted to be. No apologies. Always did what you wanted, and fuck what anyone ever told you."

Lil snorted, rolling her eyes. "And look where it got me—pregnant at seventeen. Not that I regret it," she added quickly. "I love my daughter more than anything, but it definitely wasn't easy having a baby at such a young age. Still, thank god I didn't have to raise her around Vivian." Lilian refused to call their mother by anything but her first name. "Even though it was Adam, and it was far less than satisfactory, at least you've had sex in the last decade. Do you know the last time I got laid?"

"Last weekend?" Marlina smiled.

"*Har, har.*" Lilian made a face at her. "Come on, spill."

"I think we need more wine for this." Marlina filled both their glasses to the brim and took a large swig of hers immediately. "Just because it was bad, didn't mean it happened all the time. The times we had sex were few and far between, which I was extremely grateful for after a while."

"Why 'after a while'?" Frowning, Lil opened the cast iron over door.

Immediately, the scent of marinara sauce and cheese filled the air. "Making *parmigiana, Caprese Salad, Crescenza, and prosciutto*…what's the occasion?" Changing the subject to tonight's dinner was perfect because Lilian was easily distracted by food, and the last thing she wanted to talk about was her and Adam's non-existent sex life.

"There's no occasion. I just felt like making you a nice dinner."

Liar! Marlina thought to herself. It was evident in the way she was avoiding her gaze. "And why so much wine if it's just me, you, and Nonna?" she asked, reaching up and fingering the dried herbs hanging from the oversized, hanging cast iron rack.

Groaning, Lilian looked over her shoulder. "All right, but don't say anything because I'm not supposed to tell you."

"Tell me what?" she asked, eyeing her suspiciously.

"Nonna ran into Mia at the market this morning."

"What?!" Marlina squealed, jumping up and down. "I thought she was in Greece on her second honeymoon." It was very important to Mia's husband to keep the romance in their relationship alive and show her affection, especially since Mia was pregnant with their second child and feeling less than sexy for her hot as sin husband, as she put it. Marlina didn't know why she worried, if she could see how that man looked at her, she'd know that he was totally in love and completely devoted to her. No other woman would turn his head.

Laughing, Lilian shook her head. "She just got back."

"So, this is the big secret you two have been hiding from me all day? My best friend is back in town, and she didn't even tell me. I just talked to her two days ago." Marlina arrived in Italy after Mia was off on her vacation. Mia was pissed that she didn't tell her that she was showing up, she would've postponed the trip for a few days, but Marlina didn't exactly plan this. It was spur of the moment, and by definition, that didn't really give one time to prepare anyone for anything.

"Well—"

She didn't like the hesitation or the way Lil was refusing to meet her gaze. "Lil," Marlina said sternly.

"What?"

"Out with it."

"Okay, look it, wasn't my idea...well, mostly not my idea."

Crossing her arms over her chest, she leaned her hip against the solid oak kitchen table her grandfather made the last year he was alive. It was adorned with roses and had the date of her grandparent's marriage engraved along the side. It was her grandmother's pride and joy. Marlina caught her yesterday morning, drinking coffee and talking to her grandfather with a smile on her face. Lil said it was something she did often, making her feel like he was still around waiting for her. It was the kind of love Marlina always wanted, but maybe that kind of love wasn't made for everyone.

"Spill it," she demanded.

"Well, Nonna may have also dropped by next door and invited the twins and their grandmother, but she's out of town, so it will just be Mia and the twins." She chuckles nervously.

Marlina gasped, her heartbeat speeding up. "Gabriel," she whispered. *Holy shit, the last time I saw him was the summer I turned fifteen, nearly twenty years ago.* For such a young man, he was tall and heavily muscled. He was the stuff of wet dreams for any teenage girl.

That summer, there were a lot of older ladies looking at him too, and since he'd turned eighteen, he was fair game. It was so stupid the way they fawned all over him. Besides, who did they think they were fooling—they'd been staring at him since he was sixteen, always biting their lips as he walked by. It's not like it was a secret. Not that she could blame them, she'd harbored several fantasies about her best friend's brother.

"Yeah, Nonna thought since you were all so close when you were younger that you might like to see them."

"*Oh, mi maldito dios,*" she muttered in Spanish because she didn't know enough Italian to curse like she wanted. Running her fingers through her hair, she shook her head. "I can't see him."

"Why not?" Lilian asked in confusion.

"What do you mean, why not?" Running her hands up and down her figure and then over her hair again, she sighed. "I'm a mess."

"Yeah, but a hot mess," Lilian cackled.

Narrowing her eyes at her sister, Marlina grabbed her wine, gulped it down, and poured another glass. "This isn't funny. You know I had the biggest crush on him growing up."

"Well, then it's pretty awesome that he'll be joining us for dinner in about an hour."

"What?!" she screeched. "An hour? And you're just now telling me this?"

Lilian turned her around and slapped her ass. "Better get out of those depressing clothes and into the shower and do something with that hair." Whistling, she got back to preparing dinner. "I laid something out on my bed," she hollered over her shoulder.

Rubbing her behind, she turned to her sister, arching a brow. "Just how much thought have you given this?"

Glancing over her shoulder, Lil gave a sly smile. "I don't know what you mean."

"Sure, you don't," Marlina grumbled as she dashed out of the kitchen and up the stairs.

Drawing in a deep breath and blowing it out slowly, she made her way over to the balcony that gave her a great view of the vineyard next door. So many times, over the last few days, Marlina had stood out on her balcony, remembering the sweet stolen moment between her and Gabriel the last summer she was here. It was the twin's birthday party, and they were the center of attention, Gabriel especially. He could've spent his time with anyone he wanted to that day, but he chose to ask her to take a walk with him. Stunned, but completely ecstatic, she'd agreed.

As they walked, she rambled on nervously about things she couldn't even remember now. She did remember every step they took, every smile he gave her, and she remembered when he grabbed her hand and pulled her from under the shade of a willow tree and into the vineyard. She remembered the feel of his soft lips against hers as he kissed her sweetly, and the feel of his tongue as it slid along hers. She could still remember the feel of his hard body as he pressed against her, one big hand clasping her hip, the other cupping her cheek. It was her first kiss, and she felt so clumsy, but he was patient and kind, kissing her over and over again until she no longer thought about what she was doing and melted against him.

They had stayed away from the party as long as they could, but sadly, they had to return before anyone came looking for them. They'd made plans to sneak away with each other the next day, but her mother had put her ass on a plane back to America that night Two weeks earlier than planned. Something big was going to happen that day…she could feel it. Had she stayed, she would've lost her virginity that day, she was certain of it. She never wouldn't have told him no. It would've been way better than losing her virginity to her stupid ex-husband. Unfortunately, once again, because of her mother, she'd missed out on something she wanted.

Twenty years was a long time, and here she was thinking about that day like it had happened yesterday. She was just a girl, the childhood friend of his little sister, that he had kissed once when he was a young man.

He probably doesn't even remember anything about me. Marlina didn't know if

TUSCAN HEAT

that made her feel better or worse.

TUSCAN HEAT

Chapter 2

Holding out her arms, Marlina gazed at her reflection in the oak cheval mirror that gave her a head to toe view. Intricately carved roses and twisting ivy wrapped around the wooden frame of the mirror and the stand. Gingerly, she ran her fingers along her grandfather's carvings. It was her favorite item in the whole house.

The dress on her bed fit perfectly, just as Lilian had promised. The white material made her sun-kissed tan stand out more and the cinched in the waist just below her breast made her look thinner, and her breast perky. The skirt was flaring out into a loose skirt. They were eating outside tonight, so the light, airy material would keep her cool.

Opting to keep things simple and natural, she chose to do her make up light sticking with earth tones and lip gloss. Her eyeliner and mascara really made her eyes pop against the brown eye shadow. One thing she was eternally grateful for was age perfect makeup; it didn't settle into the fine lines. She gathered up her hair that hung down to her mid-back and twisted into in a loose, romantic bun at the base of her neck held by a beautiful burgundy rose.

All in all, not bad, she thought with a smile. Suddenly, her smile faltered as a thought struck her. What if Gabriel had a girlfriend and she was coming with him to dinner? Groaning, she pressed her hand to her stomach and closed her eyes. *God, why did I listen to my damn sister and get dressed up? You're only going to embarrass yourself,* isn't that what Adam always used to say?

No matter how hard she tried to look elegant, or pretty, Adam always found something wrong with her appearance. His reasoning for pointing it out? Simple—she just wasn't very beautiful, and he didn't want her to embarrass herself and keep trying for something she was never going to achieve.

Shit, this is a terrible idea.

KNOCK! KNOCK! "What in the heck is taking you so long, Auntie Lina?" Rebekah asked, poking her strawberry blond head into the room. "*Dio mio, Zia! Sei bellissima.*"

She frowned, turning to face her niece. "My Italian is a bit rusty, kiddo."

Her full lips pulled up into a radiant smile. *God, she is the spitting image of Lil,* Marlina thought to herself as she took in the beautiful girl's appearance. "I said, you look beautiful."

Lina shook her head. "No," she said, her palms beginning to sweat. "Tell your mom I can't..."

"Can't what?" Lilian asked, popping in behind her daughter.

Releasing a shaky breath, Marlina continued shaking her head. "I can't do this, Lil."

"Sweetie," she said, turning to Becca, "go downstairs and let the DeLucas' in when they ring the bell."

"*Si, Mama.*" Bouncing out the door, she thundered down the staircase.

"What's going on?" Lilian asked, walking toward her sister.

"I can't do this, Lil," she stammered again. "I can't go down there and face them—face him. I'm going to make a fool out of myself. Adam always—"

"Oh, fuck Adam," Lilian hissed, grabbing her hand. "Adam was an asshole who didn't deserve you. He was lucky you looked at him twice."

"You don't understand...the things he used to say," Marlina shuttered at the thought. "I was never good enough for him. I was an embarrassment. He used to tell me all the time."

"Of course, he did," she snorted in disgust. "He knew you were too good for him, but he couldn't have *you* knowing that."

"Right." Rolling her eyes, she ran her hands down her dress, smoothing the skirt. "I'm such a prize...that's why I had so many boyfriends."

"You didn't have a lot of boyfriends because you studied like a freakin fiend all through high school. Then you got with Adam in, what——freshman year of college?"

"Sophomore. I was too busy studying." She palmed her face. "Lord, I never realized it before."

"Realized what?" her sister asked in confusion.

"I'm such a nerd. A bonafide, serious to the bone, geek," Marlina explained.

Lilian chuckled. "A hot geek."

"Yes, you've said." Shooting her sister an irritated look, she turned back to the mirror. "I look like I'm overdoing it."

"Why, because you're not in those damn sweat pants?" Lil walked over, reached up, and adjusted the flower in her sister's hair. "You look amazing. And you don't look overdressed. You're just not used to...to—"

She cocked a dark eyebrow. "Looking nice?"

"I wasn't going to say that, but yeah. You stopped dressing up over the years. He put you down consistently, you started believing it."

"You sound like you're speaking from experience," Marlina stated, sensing the sadness in her sister's voice. It never occurred to her there might be things she didn't know about her baby sister.

"I am," Lilian whispered, stepping back. "Now, let's shake off this downer, and get downstairs. Our company tonight features two hot men. How many women can say that?" Pulling her along behind her, Lilian walked to the door. "Even if one of them is a pain in the ass."

Marlina chuckled, not having to ask who her sister was talking about. *Lucien.* According to her Nonna, the two were forever arguing about everything under the sun. They just couldn't see eye-to-eye on anything. With Lilian being the naturally free spirit that she was, and Lucien being a financial adviser who was all about order and rules, sparks were bound to fly. *It will be interesting to see them interact tonight,* she thought as a smile played at her lips. Truth be told, she had a sneaking suspicion there was something between those two, no matter how much they both said otherwise.

Unfortunately, Gabriel was a no-show at dinner. Apparently, he was held up by a business meeting about DeLuca Wines, and it was running later than he'd expected.

Meeting? Marlina thought to herself. *Does he really expect them to believe that story?* She knew what running late meant. Adam often had *'meetings'* that ran late and look how well that story ended. In her experience, late meetings had nothing to do with a meeting at all.

Blowing off this dinner to get laid was a dick move, but honestly, what man wouldn't? Sex was everything. It was even better if it wasn't with the same woman. Again, that was according to Adam. The more she thought about it, the more she realized what a douche Adam really was. Honestly,

Marlina didn't see the big deal about sex. Maybe she didn't understand because she wasn't good at it, which Adam told her often enough. He was her only experience, so it wasn't like she could call him a liar. It was fine, and even if it weren't, there was nothing she could do to change it now.

Despite Gabriel not being at dinner, Lucien updated her on everything she missed over the years. Mia couldn't make it either. The girl closing her boutique had to take her daughter to the emergency room, so Marlina planned to stop by her shop tomorrow so they could meet up.

For as long as they'd been friends, Mia always loved makeup, clothes, and mixing scents of perfume, so it was no surprise to Marlina when her best friend mentioned that she had up and opened a store, *Mia's Boutique*. From what Lucien and Lilian told her, Mia was building quite a name for herself. Mia didn't impart that information, since she'd always been modest.

Dinner outdoors was amazing, and the décor equally stunning. It could have been on the cover of a magazine about Italian living. The place settings were atop a cotton amber-colored tablecloth with embroidered poppies and white daisies. The dishes had a character all their own, some decorated with pictures of the Renaissance, while others were covered in images of fruit, peacock feathers, and olives. Lucien complimented Lilian's candle centerpieces with roses. Marlina found it curious he'd picked white roses with pink tips, Lilian's favorite but gave them to Nonna.

Hm, curious.

Sipping the last of her wine, Marlina smiled as the conversation between Lucien and Lilian turned into a debate on rules and responsibilities. Being a teen mom, who had been kicked out of the house by their mother, Lilian had always been excellent at taking responsibility. Rules? Yeah—not so much.

Marlina didn't know much about what Lucien did as a financial advisor, but she imagined it involved a lot of structure and rules. She found they're interaction very interesting. Despite Lil's denial, she knew when her sister found a man attractive. Her eyes and the flush on her cheeks told Marlina everything she needed to know. Lilian might think that he was rigid, obnoxious, and a genuine pain in her ass, but she was attracted to Lucien. No doubt about that. The only problem was that she didn't trust men. Marlina couldn't blame her for being cautious. After all, Lilian hadn't been careful in the past, and look what happened.

She had to admit, Lucien did provide some awesome eye candy in his fitted suit, which accented his broad shoulders and tall frame. His dark brown hair was slicked back, enhancing his serious features. He was the real-life image a woman conjured up when she thought of a handsome, sinfully charming man that could make her lose her head. Which was probably why Lilian spent so much time arguing with him. It was her way of keeping him at a safe distance, while keeping her panties in place.

Lilian's short and curvy figure was a good contrast for Lucien. Lilian knew how to play up her assets, drawing attention to the curves she embraced with a self-confidence that made Marlina jealous. She knew exactly what to wear and always picked the perfect hairstyle to accentuate her heart-shaped face. Tonight, for example, she was dressed in cutoff jeans and a white, flowy tank top, and her hairstyle was a chunky layered, shoulder-length bob with sweeping bangs. Where Lucien's eyes were dark and somber, Lilian's blue-greens sparkled with mischief.

Hmm, very interesting, Marlina thought to herself as she looked on.

"You can't really be this uptight, Lucien." Lilian went to pour herself another glass of wine, but found the bottle was empty. "Please excuse me; I need to go grab another bottle of wine."

"I'll do it," Marlina offered, jumping up with a smile, effectively cutting off her sister's escape. She couldn't help but chuckle at the glare thrown her way. "Finish your conversation; I'll be right back." Turning to go into the house, she nodded. *There is definitely something behind all that arguing.* Honestly, she wouldn't be surprised if the fire between them exploded into ripping each other's clothes off one day soon. The sexual tension was there; she could feel it.

Taking a deep breath, she smiled as the scent of garlic bread and herbs hung thickly in the air from the delicious dinner Lilian made. Walking through the living room, she made her way into the kitchen. She could hear the laughter mingling outside, probably from something her grandmother said to break up the vicious argument.

For the millionth time in her life, Marlina wished she were more like her sister, with her effortless self-esteem and easy-going attitude, things just seemed much easier for her. Confidence was something that just didn't come easily to Marlina, especially after Adam. And easy-going? Yeah, that was so not her. In many ways, she was more like Lucien; serious, practical, and boring.

Her mother had drilled rules into her brain since she was a young girl. *'Always strive to be better than you are. Always take everything seriously because one day, it could affect your life, and humor is just a form of conversation for the weak-minded.'* All these years later, she realized just how ridiculous her mother was. Sadly, old habits die hard.

Now that she was free of Adam, Marlina was determined to break those habits, develop new ones, and start a happy life. A life that was her own, full of what she wanted, not what her mother wanted. Before, everything was about work and putting in long hours to make partner. Here, nothing was tying her down, stopping her from pursuing her dream of being a painter or anything else she wanted to do in life. Here, she could do what she wanted. She could follow her heart, her passion, and no one could stop her. Now, she just had to find the courage to do it.

Humming softly, she walked up to the door in the hallway, leading to the kitchen, and gave it a hard push. She cried out when the door swung back at her with a loud THUNK, followed by a masculine groan from the other side.

Shit!

Slowly, she pushed the door open, her eyes widening as she took in the massive man standing behind it. His head was tilted slightly, while one large hand rubbed his forehead in a circular motion. "Oh god," she whispered. "I'm so sorry. I didn't know anyone was here," Marlina apologized, unwittingly reaching out to grab his forearm before she could stop herself. Instinctively, the muscle flexed under her fingertips. Her breathing kicked up as that inconsequential movement had heat stealing through her body, making its way down between her thighs. *I'm getting hot from a simple touch of his arm. What the hell is wrong with me?* Marlina silently reprimanded herself. This certainly had never happened before. *This man is dangerous,* she warned herself.

"*Bastardo! Fanculo me che male!,*" *Motherfucker! Fuck me, that hurt*—the man cursed, opening his eyes.

Another startled gasp escaped her lips as her gaze locked with his. Instead of chocolate-brown eyes like Lucien's, this man's eyes were gray, like the clouds after a storm. Dangerous eyes—the kind capable of seducing a woman with a mere glance.

Gabriel. Damn, he had changed a lot over the years, but the one thing that hadn't changed; he was still incredibly hot. Unlike his brother, who had arrived in a business suit, Gabriel wore a plain black t-shirt, which looked ready to burst at the seams as it stretched across his broad shoulders, muscular chest, and well-built arms. Swirling lines of what appeared to be the tips of some kind of a tribal tattoo peeked out from beneath the neckline of the black shirt.

Tattoos. She hadn't expected that. If she was being honest, it gave him a bit of a bad boy of persona. And it was hot. *I wonder how many he has under that shirt,* she thought to herself as she bit her lip. *I would certainly love to find out. I'd trace each one with my tongue.* Marlina couldn't believe the thoughts wandering through her mind as she stood there staring at him like a lunatic. Tattoos had never been her thing, but the tides are changing, and that was all because of Gabriel. Taking in the rest of his arm, Marlina could see that both arms were sleeved, intricately detailed with a mixture of designs she couldn't quite decipher. Across the back of one of his hands, he had a brilliant picture of a rose with dewdrops on its petals. The other hand featured an old-fashioned pocket watch with the words 'Stay True' tattooed across his fingers, just above his knuckles. It surprised her that it was in English, instead of Italian.

Even though they were twins, Gabriel and Lucien couldn't have looked any more different...and it wasn't just because of the clothes they wore. Unlike his brother, Gabriel's high cheekbones accentuated his eyes, while a light dusting of dark hair along his masculine jawline added to the bad boy vibe. As her eyes roved his handsome face, she found his bottom lip was much fuller than the top, and the one side curled up in the hint of a smile. She couldn't explain it, but she had the incredible urge to run her tongue over that sensuous curl. *I wonder if they're as soft as they look.*

He was even more handsome than she remembered. From what she could see, these past twenty years had been kind to him, enhancing what he had as a teen and honing it into a broad, solid man. She had no doubt her original assumption of the kind of man he'd grown into was correct. Men who looked like him, the dangerous types, were always players. One look at him, and women were sure to be falling all over him. If there were one-thing men weren't good at, it was turning down no strings attached sex. In truth, many risked everything for that brief piece of ass. Why? She didn't know, and she doubted any woman did. Maybe it was some kind of animalistic thing. Either way, she'd probably never know.

'Honey, there are sexy, hot, women out there, ones that can make a man pant and beg. Women so beautiful he would give up everything just to see her smile at him. Women with bodies so hot they could make his dick ache. And then there's you—'. Out of

nowhere, Adam's cruel words blazed through her mind, leaving her feeling self-conscious and irritated.

Wringing her hands together, Marlina tore her eyes away from his sexy ass body and stepped back. Warmth filled her cheeks, and her eyes burned. *What am I thinking, staring at him like I want to lick and bite those sensuous lips of his? Adam is right——a man like this doesn't pay any attention to women who looked like me.* For the first time that night, Marlina wished she'd stayed in her room.

Chapter 3

Gabriel rubbed his forehead as he studied the woman standing in front of him. She was breathtaking, with striking emerald green eyes. It was the first thing he noticed about anyone. His grandmother, *dio riposa la sua anima,* also said eyes were the window to a person's soul, and he believed it too. He'd seen these eyes before, a long time ago. Twenty years to be exact. The last time on his eighteenth birthday.

His heart rate kicked up, breathing quickened, and his stomach twisted into knots. *Marlina,* he thought in amazement. He thought he'd been prepared to see her again but damn was he wrong. She was sexier than he remembered. After he heard of her marriage, he thought he lost her for good. Yet, here she was, divorced and available again. *Destino* was trying to tell him something, and he was listening.

Gabriel tracked his gaze down those sinfully sexy curves that were making his mouth water and his hands itch to trace. So enticing even under the flowy tank dress she wore. The white material looked amazing against her smooth, sun-kissed, olive-colored skin. Her skin looked satiny smooth, and he was desperate to run his fingers over her flesh and see if she was as soft as she looked. In truth, he wanted to taste every inch of her. Those long, shapely legs would feel like heaven wrapped around his waist, her heels pressing into his ass, urging him to fuck her faster and harder. His eyes continued downward, his lips curved into a smile, her feet were bare, just like when they were kids.

Curling his fingers into his palm, he squeezes tight to prevent himself from wrapping his hands around her hips and yanking her against him. The urge was nearly overwhelming. It didn't shock him. His body had always responded to her like this. Shooting through him like an electric wire, waking up every part of him, bring out the alpha male in him and making him want to take her every way he could think of. He felt possessive, which was something he never felt over a woman. Usually, he didn't care what they did or who they were with once their fun was over. Marlina was different. Had always been different. It was why he spent all those months trying to track her down only to be turned away time and time again by her mother. Some years later, she got married, and it felt like his life had ended.

Taking a deep breath, Gabriel pushed those thoughts to the back of his mind. It didn't matter, that was the past. They were starting a new chapter now, and this time she wasn't going to get away from him. No one was going to stop him from getting what he wanted, what he always wanted. This woman from the time he laid eyes on her at fifteen, he just knew she was meant to be his, taken away, and then give back. Destiny didn't always come knocking twice, and he was sure as hell wasn't going to be shy about his intentions.

He wasn't a man accustomed to waiting, and his patience was less than stellar. When he wanted a woman, he made it known, but this was Marlina. He couldn't come at her aggressively. She'd just shy away from him. No, unlike most of the women he took to bed, she would take some coaxing and seducing before she gave into him, and that's why she was, and had always been perfect for him.

Running his gaze up her body, he lingered on her full breasts, imagining them filling his hands perfectly. His gaze traveled up until his eyes connected with hers again. Those high cheekbones accentuated her face giving her an exotic look and coupled with that mouth…blow job lips. He imagined those lips wrapped around his cock so many times. How many times had he imaged her crying out in ecstasy while he pounded into her in every position imaginable? His cock stirred. Fuck, he couldn't think like that. The last thing he needed was to stand here with a fucking hard-on like a damn teenager. Shifting uncomfortably, he forced those thoughts out of his head.

At fifteen, Marlina had been shy and a little too serious, but even then, she'd been stunning…sexy and bewitching in an innocent way that was absent from the women who usually hung around him. She'd been his sister's best friend, so she was always around. He'd noticed her from the moment he saw her. She intrigued him because she never gave him the time of day. Not until that last summer. His attraction and need for her had been something he'd struggled to shake, even after all these years. He thought about her often, wondering where she was in life, what she was doing. He knew she was married, but he still wondered if she ever thought about him. Then, just like that, she was back, standing right here in front of him.

Gabriel took her hand in his. "*Ciao,* Marlina." He brushed his lips over the back of her knuckles, a tingle of awareness shooting down his spine.

She tried to tug her hand back, but he refused to let her go. "Hello, Gabriel."

"I'm glad to see you've come back to visit us. It's been a long time." He smiled again, trying to put her at ease.

Her cheeks pinkened as she quickly dropped her gaze. "It's been a long time," she agreed, almost inaudibly.

Still a little shy, just like I remember. Brushing his thumb back and forth across the back of her hand, he watched as goosebumps came to life across her skin. Satisfaction coursed through him. It might have been a long time, but she still responded to him the same just as strong as she always had.

"How long are you here for?" he asked. This time when she pulled her hand, he let her go.

"A while." She reached up, patting her hair, ensuring every hair was still in place. It was tied in a loose, romantic bun with a big burgundy flower at the back of her neck.

He pulled his mind away from how seductive she looked. The last thing he needed was for his cock to get a mind of its own again. "How are you finding everything?"

Marlina unwittingly fingered the delicate silver necklace she wore around her neck and smiled. "It's exactly like I remember. Still has the same energy about it."

"Meaning?"

She shrugged. "I don't know. It's always felt so free, less constrictive. It always makes me feel like anything is possible here."

He lowered his voice, seductive, sensual suggestion lacing his every word. "Anything is possible. Perhaps, I can show you."

Her gaze shot up to his, breath hitching. "Excuse me?"

Another smile, pouring every ounce of his charm into it. "*Castagneto Carducci* is beautiful this time of year. There are many things to do, and the beach is nearby, but I'm sure you remember all that. I'm assuming you still have a love for ancient architecture," Gabriel stated, rather than asked.

"Yes, I do," she replied, laughing softly. It was a beautiful sound he vowed to elicit from her more often. "I haven't had a chance to see any over the years, but I love it just as much as I ever did."

"Nothing's really changed since you were here last, but I don't remember you exploring the town a lot before." Marlina was always running around with Mia, that's what he remembered most. "There are many things I could show you." *And I'm not just talking about structures and ruins,* he thought to himself. "There are quite a few festivals coming up in the next month or so, if you're still around."

Biting her luscious bottom lip, she nodded. "I'll still be around." Twisting her fingers together nervously, she ducked past him into the kitchen. "I told Lil I'd get the wine. She's probably wondering what's keeping me."

"I'm sure she's too busy arguing with Lucien to even notice much else." He lifted the bottle of wine he held in his hand. "I've brought you a bottle of my *Sangiovese* wine."

"Oh yeah, I heard you took over the business after...after..." her words trailed off, no doubt because of the dark look he felt changing his features.

Pressing his lips together, he looked down at the gray stone floor. His father was still a sore subject for him, one he didn't particularly like talking about. Marlina didn't know about his father's philandering, or the fact that he used to take his sons to his mistress's house, leaving them outside in the car, while he went in for a few hours. His father would give him and his brother money and instruct them on what to say to their mother when they returned home. His father took them with him to cover his ass, so his wife wouldn't find out about his various lovers. Gabriel never spent one cent of that money. In fact, he dropped it in the donation box at church.

"Lucien and I inherited it after my parent's divorce," he explained, keeping his voice steady and calm.

Taking a deep breath, she ran her finger across the smooth pine island in the middle of the spacious kitchen. "I'm sorry, Gabriel. I didn't mean to bring up bad memories."

Reaching for the corkscrew by her hand, he gave her a small smile. "*Va bene."* He'd talk about anything in his life, even something as distasteful as his father, if it meant she'd keep talking to him. "Our history is what makes us who we are. Besides, it's how I came to inherit the vineyard, something I've wanted since I was a child."

"How come your father didn't maintain control of it?" Marlina asked.

It made him feel good that she was comfortable enough to ask personal questions. That just showed him that she trusted him on some level, even if she didn't know it yet. "My father lost everything in the divorce—due to his infidelity."

She frowned, tilting her head to the side. "I don't understand," she said in confusion. "When your parents were married, wasn't it common for a man to have multiple affairs? Even expected?"

"It was in their marital agreement. My grandmother had the good sense to have it stipulated in the prenup. If he didn't agree, she wouldn't give her blessing." Pressing the metal point into the cork, he began twisting, driving the spiral screw into the soft material. This bottle of Sangiovese was ten years old, and the musty, rustic scent was heady, while the fruity taste was perfect for a warm night, much like tonight.

He continued. "My mother and father were an arranged marriage. She knew there was a fifty-fifty chance my father would stay faithful to her. She likely would not have asked for the clause, had it been up to her, but since it wasn't, she didn't fight it." Pulling the cork out, he brought the bottle up to his nose and breathed deep. *Delizioso.* Many people mistakenly believe a dry wine meant the absence of flavor, but there's plenty of flavor…nice, smooth, fruity taste. It didn't taste like damn fruit juice, like so many women he dated favored.

I wonder if Marlina will be the same, or if she will appreciate the bold, fruity flavor like I do.

"Why did she marry him?" she asked, straightening. "I'm sorry, I shouldn't have asked."

He shook his head. "No. It's all right. To answer your question, it was expected of my mother," he sighed, pouring the wine. "It wasn't in her to go against her *famiglia*." Holding the glass out to her, Marlina wrapped her slender fingers around the stem. "It was easier for her to go along with what my grandfather wanted. You see, in those days, things were different. Thankfully, they've changed for the better now. I, for one, am glad for it." Holding up his glass, he clanked it against hers. "To old friends."

"To old friends," she whispered, taking a deep drink of the wine. Closing her eyes, she ran her tongue across her lips and leaned against the island.

Suppressing a groan, his body jerked forward of its own accord. Barely able to control himself, he had to grasp the counter to keep from grabbing her. *Damn, she makes something as simple as drinking wine look like the most erotic thing I've ever seen.*

"Gabriel?" Marlina asked, drawing his attention back to her.

Jerking his gaze up to meet hers, he swallowed hard. "*Sí?*"

Smiling, she gently swished the wine in her glass in a circular motion. "I said, maybe we should go outside and join everyone else."

He nodded, unable to say anything else because his mouth had gone dry, and his tongue was sticking to the roof of his mouth. He was certain of one thing, this woman was going to be his. She belonged *to him, with him*, and he was going to have her—just as he should've all those years ago.

Marlina could feel Gabriel's gaze burning into her back as they made their way outside onto the veranda. Embarrassment warred with feminine pride at being the focus of his attention. Her cheeks grew warm, and despite her reservations, her ass shook a little more than usual. He was totally checking her out, and she couldn't help but like it.

There's nothing wrong with wanting his eyes on me, she told herself. Besides, it wasn't like she'd hold his attention for very long. Just until a younger, prettier chick caught his attention, isn't that what Adam always said? *Shit. Adam.* She needed to get him out of her head, or she'd be acting like a mental case for the rest of her life. Whatever Adam thought it was just the opinion of one man.

When Gabriel and Marlina stepped out onto the veranda, Nonna was laughing at something Lucien was saying. She couldn't help but notice he looked more comfortable with his sleeves rolled up to just above his elbows, and a few buttons undone as he poured another round of the white wine that had been left. Lilian was standing up, reaching for his plate as she talked. Lucien couldn't have been paying attention to a word she said because his gaze was glued to her chest, right where her shirt gaped open as she leaned over the table, which gave him a perfect shot of her cleavage.

"Gabriel," Nonna exclaimed, jumping to her feet as he walked over to her.

"*Come stai?*" He asked charmingly, bending down to kiss her cheek. "I wrapped up my meeting as quickly as possible. There wasn't a chance I was going to miss this dinner. Not with Lilian cooking."

"*Grazie,*" Lilian said, sticking her tongue out at Lucien before smiling brightly at Gabriel. "I packed some up just for you." Her gaze flickered to Marlina, and her smile grew even bigger. "Where did you two run into each other?"

"In the kitchen," Marlina offered, sitting down.

"She hit me with the door," Gabriel stated matter of factly as he rubbed his forehead and winked.

Marlina's lady bits did a little dance at his attention. Dear God, she was on the verge of panting from that wink. Was she really this pathetic? So, starved for attention that just a wink from this man was getting her all hot? Looking over at Gabriel once again, she chuckled, *Yup.*

"Marlina?" Lilian whispered, leaning in closer.

Ignoring her sister, she focused on the exquisite glass of *Sangiovese* in her hands. It was a full-bodied red wine, the first splash of flavor being tart cherries. Closing her eyes, Marlina imagined walking through the market in the piazza—the scent of dried oregano and other herbs hanging thickly in the air. Somewhere in the crowd, a barista brewed several cups of espresso, making the air thick with the scent of aromatic coffee scent. In the corner, an elderly man puffed on a pipe, filling the air with the heady scent of tobacco. Yes, this *Sangiovese* tasted like Italy.

Just then, a sharp pain brought her back to reality. "Ouch," she hissed, rubbing her arm as she glared at her sister. "Why did you pinch me?"

Lilian smirked. "What happened?"

"I didn't know he was in the kitchen," she muttered. "So, I pushed the door open, and it..." Her sister burst into uncontrollable laughter. "What? Why are you laughing?"

"Because you're so damn accident-prone, it's sad."

Shaking her head, she stuck her tongue out at her. "Bite me." Turning her attention back to Lucien, Nonna, and Gabriel, she instantly regretted it. All three of them had their eyes trained on her. "What?" she asked.

"*Scusami?*" Her grandmother frowned. "What did you just say?"

A flush crawled up her cheeks. "Um—nothing, Nonna. I was just—just–"

"Telling me about her job," Lilian piped up, supplying a topic for a diversion.

Marlina shot her a dirty look. *Out of all the things to bring up right now, she has to bring up my damn job.*

"*Veramente?*" Nonna clasped her hands together. "I've been asking you about your job since you arrived. *Per favore*, tell us about your work."

Lucien nodded in agreement. "It's been so long since we've seen you, Marlina, but Mia tells us you went to Columbia University to study law, right?"

She felt like a deer in headlights. "What?"

Gabriel cocked his head to the side, his gaze becoming more intense than before. "What do you do back in the States?" He looked interested and curious, but she had a feeling it wasn't about her job.

"I—ummm. Well—" she stammered before giving a nervous, high-pitched laugh. Panicking, she looked to Lil for help.

Never one to leave her treading thin ice alone, Lilian cleared her throat. "My bad, everyone. I shouldn't have said that. We weren't really talking about her job—Lina doesn't have a job anymore. Isn't that right?" she asked, looking to Marlina for confirmation.

Glancing at her hands in her lap, she nodded. "I quit."

"*Perché?*" Poor Nonna sounded so confused now.

"I never wanted to be a lawyer, Nonna," she admitted.

"Vivian," Lilian supplied, her face scrunching up at the mention of their mother.

"Who's Vivian?" Lucien asked, turning his attention to Lilian.

"Our mother," she scowled. "She'd had a plan for Lina's life ever since she was born."

Marlina looked from her sister to her grandmother, to Gabriel, and back to her grandmother. "They were going to make me partner, and I had this awful feeling I was going to be stuck forever." Much like how she felt in her marriage with Adam. Taking a deep breath, she shook her head. "I left everything behind, and I'm not going back. I know I should've told you, Nonna, but I—"

"*No, ragazza mia.*" Nonna always referred to Marlina as her girl since she was a young child. It always touched something inside her, and right now, the sentiment had her gaze blurring. "There's nothing to apologize for. Your life is your own, no one else's."

Choking back a sob, the loud sound of metal scraping against the concrete echoed as she pushed her chair back and jumped to her feet. "Please, excuse me." She ran from the room, escaping just as the first of the tears fell. Out of all the times for the horrible mess that was her life to come out, it had to be when Gabriel was here.

Mortification flooded her as she slammed her bedroom door shut. Leaning against it, she closed her eyes, silent tears falling. Now here she was, thirty-six years old, divorced, and out of a job she had spent her whole life working towards. And if all that change weren't enough, she'd uprooted herself from America and had no intention of going back. It was pretty intense when three major life changes all happened in the same week. Aside from the train wreck that was her life, she only had one question—*Where do I go from here?*

How had everything gotten so messed up? Why did I let my mother rule my life for so long? And why did I just word vomit it all over everyone at dinner? She thought as sobs shook her body. Gabriel probably wouldn't want to talk to her again after that embarrassing scene.

TUSCAN HEAT

Chapter 4

Groaning, Marlina rolled onto her back. Throwing her arm over her eyes, she tried to block out the bright sunshine pouring in from the open doors to her balcony. She loved the outdoors and enjoyed the sun, but right now, she hated it.

Her head was pounding, and the bright sunshine felt like shards of glass were being shoved into her eyes. *Damn.* Why did she drink so much and then cry herself to sleep?

After the train wreck that dinner turned out to be, all she wanted was to stay in bed and sleep all day, but it wasn't an option. If she stayed in bed today, she'd do the same thing tomorrow, and the next day and so on. Besides, she owed her grandmother an explanation, or five.

Opening her eyes, she squinted. Tossing the sheet from her body, she swung herself to a sitting position on the edge of the bed. Her grandfather always said to keep putting one foot in front of the other. And at the moment, it was the only advice she could focus on. Expecting anything else just seemed like asking too much. Resting her face against the palm of her hands, a wave of nausea washed over her, and her stomach somersaulted. Pulling in a deep breath through her nose, she tried to push down the bitter taste coating her mouth.

Fuck hangovers.

KNOCK! KNOCK!

"Come in," she said. Hearing the door open, she opted not to raise her head.

A loud chuckle filled the air. "Boy, don't you look like chocolate on a hot summer's day." Lilian always did have a way with metaphors.

"Thanks a lot, she grumbled.

"Wanna talk about it?" she asked, her voice concerned.

Shaking her head slowly, Marlina stood up and walked into the bathroom. "Not really, but I doubt that's going to stop you."

"Good guess." Lilian clucked her tongue, propping her shoulder against the wall. "Why'd you spill your guts last night?"

Shrugging, Marlina stared at herself in the vanity mirror. "Why does it seem like we deteriorate through the night, and men wake up looking perfect?"

"Just one more thing for us to hate them for," Lil muttered before walking over to stand beside her. "Now, you wanna tell me what the hell happened last night?" she pressed.

"Nothing." Turning on the cold water, she braced her hands on the porcelain bowl and stared down into the drain. The water swirled around and around until it was finally sucked down. "Look, Nonna deserved to know the truth."

"And Gabriel?"

Frowning, she turned her head slightly to look at her sister. "It had nothing to do with him."

"No?"

"Look, Lil, I suck at hints right now. So, if there's something you want to tell me, then just spit it out, okay?"

"Fine. Are you sure you didn't do that whole life fact, word vomit shit to scare Gabriel off?" she asked knowingly.

Guilt snaked through her. "No," she denied.

Lilian was always way too perceptive for her own good, raised a brow in speculation. "You really expect me to buy that bullshit answer?"

"I don't care what you buy." Reaching over, Marlina turned on the shower. "I told you, I didn't do...you know what, it doesn't matter."

"I bet it does."

"Leave it alone," she snapped, having enough of the conversation and whatever truth Lilian figured she stumbled upon. Granted, she did know the truth, but that was beside the point. "I'm not here to find a man, Lil." *Least of all, an insanely hot one who is way out of my league.* "Now, do you mind?"

Narrowing her eyes, Lilian turned to the door. "Fine, but don't think you've escaped. We're coming back to this."

"The hell we are," Marlina mumbled, stripping off her nightshirt.

"I want to know why you are deliberately sabotaging yourself," Lilian said before walking out and closing the door behind her.

Some things are none of anyone's business, and this was one of them. The last thing she needed was to get twisted up over a man from her past. There was no way she was going to see Gabriel again. If she did happen to run into him, she would be polite but not too polite. She didn't want him to keep coming around.

Liar, the annoying voice in her head screamed.

Stupid voice.

Whoever said that *'hair of the dog that bit ya'* had it absolutely right. Marlina heard the saying plenty of times in her life, but she'd never tried it. Looking too bright, and far too cheerful, Lilian bounded into the kitchen to inform her they were going into town to visit Mia at her store. Marlina had intended to put it off until tomorrow. Not because she wasn't anxious to finally see her best friend in person after all these years of being apart, but she felt like shit. After seeing the look on her face, Lil suggested she have a glass of wine to feel better. It was weird because back home, it was something, she'd never even think about doing, probably because it would piss her mother off. Here, it seemed perfectly reasonable, it would make her feel better and help her get on and enjoy the day.

One thing about Italy and alcohol was that everyone drank wine and they drank it all day. Not to get drunk, it was just part of their culture and served at every meal. Even children got exposed to it from an early age, so there was no great mystery to them as they got older. If there was no big mystery, then they were less likely to binge drink like kids in the U.S.

Making their way into town, Marlina couldn't help but notice how it was so easy for her to forget her problems here. There was no pressure, no pushing, no rushing, and really no expectations. Things just seemed to coast here. It was one of the most picturesque places she'd ever been. Slopes of green hills were dusted with deep purples and reds from wild lavender and violets. Rows and rows of vines stretched up the rolling hills and extended far into the distance with all the splendor and majestic beauty of a Rembrandt painting.

Passing a little bistro, she watched as a man got down on one knee and popped the question to his shocked lover. The man had his hands pressed against his mouth, shoulders shaking as he sobbed with happiness, nodding his acceptance. Jumping to his feet, the other man embraced his love, and they shared a passionate kiss that almost made her blush. The small medieval town was the perfect place for romance; there was no denying that.

As they made their way toward Mia's Boutique, the sweet scent of baking pastries wafted around Marlina, distracting her from the happy couple. Instinctively, her stomach growled. *Too bad I'm staying away from pastries,* she thought sadly. She needed to lose a few pounds, something else Adam used to tell her. It was something she happened to agree with, and not because Adam was still stuck in her head. She'd made a decision last night, whatever actions Adam had suggested, she would do the opposite.

She sighed happily, despite denying herself delicious puffs of sweet bread. Her life could be different here. It could be the life she wanted, a life she was happy with—truly happy. *Have I ever been truly happy?* The answer was obvious…no. Marlina never had the kind of happiness the couple in the bistro had, or the barista in the coffee shop, or even the people tossing pennies into the wishing fountain.

"You know," Lilian said, pulling open the door to Mia's Boutique. "You never talked to me about Adam."

Marlina frowned. "What do you mean?" Glancing around, she looked for the best friend she hadn't seen for forever. "Where's Mia?"

"She said she was in the back talking to an employee, and she'd be out in a minute," Lilian said, putting her phone away. "We used to talk about everything when you were living in the U.S.—your job, coworkers, clients that were pissing you off, even that cute guy who flirted with you on the subway. You never talked about your life with Adam. Ever."

"There wasn't anything to mention," she stated flatly. "I never saw him. We lived separate lives for so long that sometimes I forgot we were even married. We were more like roommates than husband and wife. What was I supposed to say?"

"That."

Marlina shook her head and sighed. "Then you would've had all kinds of questions, and…." her voice trailed off.

"And what?"

"You know what, Lil," she said, turning to look through a rack of shirts.

"Obviously, I don't, so why don't you tell me."

"You would've begged me to tell you exactly what was wrong, and what was happening. Then you would've called Adam to chew his worthless ass out, even if I begged you not to."

"Damn right, I would've." She didn't bother denying it as she took a yellow sundress with daises off the rack and handed it to Marlina. "A man shouldn't ignore his wife, especially when she is trying so hard. Shit, you can stay single for that."

"Shhh," she hissed, looking around the store. "Don't curse. Besides, I wasn't trying all that hard. At all, actually."

Lilian's delicate brows rose. "What?"

"There were a lot of things I was looking for where Adam was concerned, but a connection wasn't one of them."

"Come again?" Lilian couldn't have looked more shocked if she stripped off her shirt and ran around the Boutique dancing.

Marlina sighed dejectedly. "I didn't care about the distance between us anymore. I mean, at first, I did, but then it just faded away. He was constantly telling me how disappointing I was in my career, my looks, my friends, everything. Nothing I did could ever please him. The less he was home, the more I was by myself, and the happier I was."

"Then why were you so devastated about the divorce?"

"Certainly not for the reasons you're thinking."

"So, tell me," she said, curious.

Just then, a loud, feminine squeal sounded from the back of the store.

"Marlina!"

Turning in the direction of the voice, Marlina spotted a petite blond rushing through the store just before being enveloped in a tight embrace. Glancing over her shoulder at Lilian, who was still frowning speculatively, she shot her sister a stern look. Her damn divorce wasn't a conversation she was anxious to have when she was in such a happy mood and feeling better than she had in a long time.

Closing her eyes tightly, Marlina hugged Mia tighter and soaked up all the feels that she'd been missing for the woman that was such a good friend. They lost contact after her fifteenth birthday, the last summer she was allowed to spend here because of her mother. Vivian was nothing if not unflinchingly controlling, especially when it came to getting something she wanted and what she wanted was for Marlina to have the life that she planned out for her. She wasn't above anything to get it, including locking down Marlina's email, and her cell phone. Not to mention keeping her so busy with studying and after-school programs, she didn't have time to do anything but sleep. She lost touch with Lil after her and Adam married. She just got so busy. Work, married life, social life, things like that. Even during the first year things were strained between her and Adam. She turned to Lil, the only person she could ever talk to about anything. Her sister was always there to listen, offer advice or a shoulder to cry on. Lilian put her back in contact with Mia, and from the minute they started talking again, and they fell right back into things like no time had passed.

A very round, very hard bump pressed into her abdomen. Pulling back, she looked down, a huge smile dancing across her lips. Cupping the sides of her belly, she grinned. "I can't believe I'm actually here to see it this time. I'm so excited. Have you had a baby shower yet?"

Mia shook her head. "No. I've still got a few more months to go. Plus, we put it off because of the trip. It's like my soul knew you were coming."

Mia hugged her hard again. "My dear friend, I've missed you so much. I'm so glad you're back." Pulling back, she looked her over from head to toe, her eyes sparkling with delight. "You look amazing. How long are you staying?"

"Forever," Lilian interjected from over her shoulder.

Mia's eyes widened, and giddiness took over. "Really?"

Marlina laughed and nodded. "Really. I'm not going back to America."

"*Oh, mio dio,*" she squealed. "This is the best present ever. My best friend is not only going to be here for the birth of my second child, but she's going to be living here." Mia jumped up and down. "This is so wonderful. Oh, oh." She stopped pressing her hand to her belly. "I better stop. She gets all wound up and won't stop kicking for hours."

"How's Luke and Jr.?" Marlina asked.

"Good. Luke's job keeps him pretty busy, but he always makes time for us." She rubbed her belly, smiling wistfully. "Jr. is just like his father." She rolls her eyes.

"Oh, so he's a charmer then too?"

"More like a troublemaker," Mia laughed. "But he is an *ammaliatore*, which he gets from his *papà* too. Spitting image too*, mio dio.*" Grabbing her hand, Mia pulled Marlina along behind her as she maneuvered through the racks of clothing. "Now, Lilian tells me you need a new *armadio.*"

"A what?" Marlina asked, unsure of what her friend had just said.

"Wardrobe," Lilian piped up. "Desperate need," Lilian clarified. Marlina shot her a dirty look, but her sister just shrugged. "You do."

"Thanks for being willing to do what my deranged sister suggests, but I'm fine with the clothes I have." She wasn't. At least, not if she wanted to look like a woman and not like some stuffy lawyer. However, she was embarrassed to admit her clothing was lacking.

Lilian snorted. "No, you're not."

"I am too," Marlina argued, her voice laced with irritation.

"Everything is beige," Lilian countered, quirking her brow. "Is that how you want to dress? Do you think that's going to catch any man's attention?" Lilian certainly wasn't afraid to poke holes in her image. "I mean, most of your clothing is business attire," she added.

Marlina opened her mouth to deny it but couldn't. It was true. Not only were the clothes she brought with her similar in color and style, but so were all the ones she'd gotten rid of before she left New York. *Do I really dress that drab?* Shit, no wonder no man ever looked her way; she wasn't giving them much to drool over.

Her mother always pushed her to dress more conservatively, even when she was younger. *'Dress serious, be taken seriously,'* Vivian would say. It was her motto, and something she drilled into Marlina's head for so long that she hadn't even realized that it became something she lived by her entire life.

Well, I came to Tuscany for a makeover, so it might as well start here. This was her new life, and she was exhilarated to find the new her.

Grabbing a white sundress with daisies and purple violets all over it, she smiled. "Yellow isn't my color. I like this one, though. What do you think?" she asked, holding it up next to her. The dress hit her just above her knee, and the material was light and flowy.

Lilian nodded. "Yes." Pushing Marlina toward the dressing room, she said, "Now try it on before you lose your nerve."

"I'm not going to lose my nerve. I'm the one who picked it out." She opened her mouth to say something else, but Lilian cut her off.

"Great." Lilian waved her hand in a shooing motion, "I'll look for some shoes."

Suspicion rolled through Marlina, making her wary. Something told her that her sister was up to something, but she didn't have a clue what. Heading in the direction of the dressing room, she found a small room about the size of a closet, closed off by what looked like a curtain on a strand of rope.

"You've got to be kidding," she muttered. Walking past the curtain, she looked around to make sure no one would be able to see her.

As she pulled the curtain shut, doubt began to set in. *Maybe this wasn't such a good idea.* Truth is, she wasn't anything like Lilian. When she was away from the ever-watchful eye of her mother, she tried to be more like her sister, many times, but it never worked. She just wasn't audacious, outgoing, or a free spirit. Getting this dress was one thing, but getting naked in the back of the store, behind a thin curtain of material was pushing her out of her comfort zone.

Turning around, she faced the large mirror hanging on the wall. Taking in the sight of her reflection, she grimaced. She was wearing a beige dress that fell just below her knees and a pair of sensible flats. It looked like an outfit she'd wear to the office. In fact, she probably had.

Yup, this was why men ignore me. Well, I'm changing all that starting now, she thought to herself, resolute in her decision.

This dress and changing in a matchbox size dressing room was the first step to taking back control of her life. Taking a deep breath, Marlina pulled the zipper down on her current dress and let it drop to the ground. It was going in the trash after today. Slipping the pretty, flowy dress on, she nearly groaned at the delicious feel of the satiny material against her skin.

Raising her gaze to the mirror, she studied herself carefully. The dress looked amazing on her, and it molded perfectly to her curves. Reaching up, she unclipped her hair and shook it out gently. Her mid-length brown locks tumbled past her shoulders in loose waves that gave her appearance a romantic quality. She tried desperately to ignore the fine lines around her eyes and the wideness of her hips, but old habits and all that jazz. She could admit she looked pretty—nothing to stop traffic, but it was a vast improvement.

Her mind drifted back to last night, and her run-in with Gabriel. She'd never seen a man quite as sexy as him, at least not up close. Seeing him for the first time after twenty years didn't go exactly how she imagined it would, but that was life. Smacking him in the head with the door wasn't the suavest way to be reintroduced to someone, but what could she do? She was clumsy as all get out, and there was no hiding that.

Her intense attraction to the man after all these years was something that shocked her almost as much as whacking him on the head. She'd thought he was cute from when they were children, but when they hit their teens, his looks transformed him. Hitting a growth spurt at sixteen, he filled out into a man that the entire female population within a fifty-mile radius drooled over.

Leaning back against the wall next to the mirror, she closed her eyes and thought back to that last summer she'd spent here in Italy. The summer when everything lined up and the boy that she'd daydreamed about kissed her for the first time.

In front of the wine table, a group of girls whispered to each other and looked over at her. She knew exactly what they were thinking, 'why was the American girl here'. She'd been spending summers in Italy for a long time but only managed to make one friend in all the years she spent here. Mia DeLuca didn't have many friends either, at least not ones that she could trust liked her for her. Most of the girls that wanted to hang out with her tried to get close to one of her brothers.

The twins, Gabriel and Lucien, were the most popular boys in town. Everyone wanted to be their friends and today was their birthday. Seemed like everyone came out to help them celebrate their eighteenth birthday. Especially the women of the town, and they were of all ages. Even some of the married ones were here giving the brothers the eye, knowing they were fair game, and had no objection to having an affair with young men.

Every relative in the DeLuca family was here. It was one of the things she loved about Italians. When they did something, they did it big, and everyone came to celebrate and show their support. She was here because Mia invited her, not wanting to be alone with all the superficial girls that were here pretending to like her but pushing to talk to the twins.

Sighing heavily, she folded her arms over her chest and headed down to the Weeping Willow tree by the small pond that separated the DeLuca property from her grandmother's place. She didn't want to be a party pooper, but it seemed wrong to stand around just staring at everyone, pretending to have a good time. She loved the pond and the massive tree with its long branches. It made for some awesome shade. It was perfect for sitting under, resting back against the trunk, and looking out over the water.

Sighing, she sat down in the lush grass by the waterline. In the distance, she saw two ducks swimming together, dipping their heads toward each other now and then. Leaning back against the rough bark of the tree trunk, she hummed lightly to herself as she watched them and imagined they were lovers. Taking care of each other and indulging in a stolen moment of affection.

Affection. There was a foreign word. Her mother never showed her affection or even hugged her often for that matter. She never even saw her mother hugging her father or her sister.

"Are you hiding down here?" A deep, masculine voice rumbled from behind her.

His voice and his accent sent shivers down her spine. Taking a breath, she told herself to relax and act like a normal person. Turning her head, she smoothed her hands down her skirt.

Smiling, she shrugged one shoulder. "Just taking a break from the crowd."

Nodding, he squatted down next to her. "It is a little crowded up there." He glanced over his shoulder, looked back at her, and rolled his eyes. "I knew some girls were coming," he muttered, plucking a piece of grass from between them.

"Didn't know all of them were coming, huh?" She chuckled.

He laughed. "You don't think I invited all of them, do you?"

Her mother had repeatedly warned her that all boys only wanted one thing and were totally ruled by their hormones. Completely incapable of making good decision. Lina also found out from her friends that the main thing boys wanted was sex. Of course, they'd want every woman in the area attending their party. Falling all over them, competing for their attention. Besides, if one female turned them down, there was another one waiting in line. It was every male's dream, but she didn't care. She was ecstatic that the boy she had a crush on forever came all the way down here just to talk to her.

"Maybe, but then I'd have to wonder why you're trying to escape your own party."

He raised his gaze to lock with hers. "Because the woman I wanted to see is down here," he said in a low voice that she was sure he used to seduce women. It seemed to be working. Her heart hammered in her chest, and her stomach tied into knots. She had the urge to squirm. It sure as hell was working on her.

Heat rushed up her neck, spreading across her cheeks. "Uh, um," she stammered. Squeezing her eyes closed, she gave her head a hard shake. Damn, she couldn't even speak right.

Real fucking smooth.

He chuckled, reaching out and taking her hand in his. "Go for a walk with me." Getting to his feet, he gently pulled her up with him.

Brushing off her butt, she glanced back at the celebration behind her. "What about the party?"

"It's my birthday," he said, pulling her along with him. "I can do what I want."

When she got nervous, she rambled and that was exactly what she was doing. Talking about everything and nothing, her brain whispering to her to just shut up. They walked around the pond to where all the vines were. They were out of sight of the party, alone, just the two of them, and Gabriel didn't let go of her hand either. The setting sun cast a pinkish-orange golden glow across the rows upon rows of perfectly manicured grapevines. They grew over the land and up the hills, stretching as far as the eye could see.

"Wow," she said, walking among the large vines. "It's so beautiful."

"Yes," he muttered, squeezing her hand gently. Stopping, he reached out and caressed a plump purple grape. She stared at his perfect, thick fingers. Such big hands, perfect hands that made her quiver, just thinking about them caressing her body. "Have you ever had grapes directly from the vine, warmed by the sun?"

In complete awe of how he could make such a simple act seem so erotic, she could only shake her head no.

Plucking the grape, he kept his gaze on her as he brought the fruit to her lips. "It's delicious," he whispered.

Staring into his eyes, she opened her mouth and took the grape, her lips brushing his fingertips. Once the skin was broken, sweet, succulent juice burst on her tongue, filling her mouth as she chewed. She had grapes before, but nothing quite like this. So succulent and delicious.

"Good, si?"

"Yes," she said, licking her lips. "I've never tasted grapes like that before."

"It's a special kind of grape. I can't tell you what kind." He tucked a strand of her dark hair behind her ear. "It's a secret."

Laughing, she looked down at their clasped hand. The air around her felt charged with electricity, and those damn butterflies were fluttered in her stomach like she was on a roller coaster. Tingles raced across her flesh, raising goosebumps over her skin. She was hyper-aware of everything that was happening, every move Gabriel made, and how his breathing had increased. Much like her own. It was one of those moments just before something big happened.

"Lina," he whispered, the callused tip of his thumb scratching gently across her cheek.

Her eyes connected with his depthless gray eyes. Her gaze drifted down to those sexy, full lips. What would it be like to kiss him? To taste him. Her attention moved to those broad shoulders before trailing over the rest of his hard body. Just eighteen, but he had the body of a man from the time he was sixteen. It was at that age that he first started turning heads of women everywhere.

He stepped closer, so close she could feel the heat from his body. So warm and strong. She looked up at him, fire burned in his gaze, making her tingle with excitement inside and out. She might be inexperienced, but she knew desire when she saw it.

"Gabriel," she whispered, as he leaned closer to her.

Smiling, he ran that callused thumb over her bottom lip. "You're so beautiful. So sweet." His gaze fell to her lips. "You know what I want, more than anything, for my birthday?"

Swallowing hard, she shook her head, unable to find her voice.

"I want to kiss you," his voice was low and husky. "Will you give me my birthday kiss Lina?" His gaze wandered back up to and locked with hers.

She couldn't believe this was happening. Something she'd thought about, dreamed about was actually happening. Her head was spinning, because yes, she'd thought about this moment, but she never thought it would happen. She didn't even know that Gabriel knew she was alive. She didn't know why he was suddenly paying attention to her, and she didn't care. Determination steeled through her; she was going to grab this moment with both hands and worry about the consequences later. He was going to be her first kiss. She wanted that. She wanted Gabriel to be her first everything.

Tilting her head back, she gave a shy smile, her bottom lip trembled slightly. "Yes," she whispered.

And he did.

TUSCAN HEAT

Chapter 5

God. She thought about that perfect moment many times over the years. When she thought about him, she figured the attraction she remembered was exaggerated because he was her first kiss. Though, based upon her experience last night, she was dead wrong. In fact, it was just as strong as she remembered, which was *so* not good. She wanted to stay away from men like Gabriel, unwilling to fall at his feet like every other woman. Those women might be okay with being used, but she'd had quite enough of a man using her to get what he wanted.

Straightening her spine, she tilted her chin. Deep down, Marlina knew the nasty thoughts she had about her appearance were from her ex. While Adam might not have been physically abusive, he certainly did plenty to keep her self-esteem low. He didn't like their marriage any more than she did, she could see that now looking back. It was something that never occurred to her but was becoming more and more clear the more she thought about her marriage. Adam wanted to please his family, much like she wanted to please her mother. That had to be it. There had to be a reason why he was so mean to her. He'd damaged her with verbal abuse over the years, but she was determined to undo it, and she was starting with this dress. Determination was what got her to the top of her class at Columbia and got her on the partner track within two years. The same steel determination was going to be what healed her from the poison her ex-husband had flooded into her mind.

Giving herself a bright smile, she nodded her head. "Not bad. Not great, but definitely not bad." She didn't exactly believe her words, but if she kept repeating them to herself, she would eventually believe them. It just took time. Everything, every change someone made, began with a single step, and she was taking her first one.

Taking a deep breath, she pulled back the curtain and walked out of the small changing room. Turning toward the central part of the store with a big smile, she was ready to show off to her sister and best friend; however, she froze immediately at the sight of the tall, broad-shouldered, sinfully attractive man standing there chatting with Lilian.

As if sensing her entrance, Gabriel's stormy gaze fell on her. Whistling softly, he ran his gaze up and down her body. "*Sei bellissima,*" he muttered, stepping forward. "You're an absolute vision."

Her heart skipped a beat, and butterflies fluttered in her tummy. *Damn, does the man have to be so sinfully sexy? And charming—with a damn accent in the sexiest language ever created?*

She smiled. "Thank you, Gabriel."

"That color brings out the flecks of gold in your eyes," he said softly as he stepped closer to her.

Her breathing grew heavier the closer he got, her palms sweating, and her heart was fluttering like a bat trapped in a cage. She felt like she was having a fucking meltdown. *It isn't like I've never talked to good-looking men before, so what the hell is wrong with me?*

"I–I don't have any gold in my eyes," Marlina stammered, clearing her throat.

"You do," he corrected. With a seductive smile, he reached out and tucked a strand of hair behind her ear, just like he had all those years ago. "When the light hits the green just right, you can see just the slightest flicker of gold around your pupils."

With a small gasp, she pressed her hand to her chest, surprised by his statement. No man had ever paid that much attention to her eyes. In fact, she was pretty sure Adam didn't even know what color her eyes were, and he was her husband.

"How do you know that?" she whispered.

He shrugged one shoulder. "*So tutto di te*," he purred.

She shook her head gently. "I don't know what that means."

Gabriel just smiled, as he took that last step bringing him inches from her chest. "I remember the last summer you were here, you were fifteen, and you wore that white sundress with the little blue flowers on it. Your hair was down, with big curls that fell down your back." He fingered her soft strands gently. "Much like it is now."

Her mouth dropped open. *He remembers that?* She hadn't expected him to remember the kiss they shared, let alone what she wore. "That's right. I can't believe you remember that."

"I've thought of that day often." A devilish glint sparkled in his eyes. "Especially when I pass that part of the vineyard."

She sucked in a quick, sharp. He remembered the kiss, their kiss, her first kiss. The one she played over and over in her head a billion times. She never felt like she did when he kissed her. Her pulse racing, stomach clenching, core aching, legs trembling, all those consuming feelings as she melted into him, and she wanted to feel them again.

"How do you remember that? It was so long ago."

His smile widened, displaying a small dimple in his left cheek. *Dimples? Did God have no mercy?* She silently cursed.

"*Non potrei mai dimenticare nulla di te. Le tue labbra dolci, le tue curve sexy—ogni centimetro di te mi ha perseguita da quando le nostre labbra si sono toccate.*". Seeing the confused look upon her face, his gaze fell to her lips. "I remember everything," he whispered.

She stared up into his eyes, speechless. Every word sounded like music; it was so beautiful.

Behind them, Lilian cleared her throat, shattering the illusion. Marlina quickly stepped back, carefully smoothing out her skirt.

"That dress looks amazing on you," Lilian said. "It fits in all the right places, and the color compliments your skin tone."

Marlina fumbled nervously with her necklace. "You really think so?"

"Absolutely," Lil whistled. "You'll get attention from all of the men around here wearing that."

Her cheeks flamed. "I don't want to get attention," she mumbled. "I just wanted something fun with a little color."

Lil chuckled. "Well, you found it. So, Marlina, Mia, needs some help with her inventory. Otherwise, she'll be here all night."

Marlina narrowed her eyes at her sister, not believing the excuse for a second. "Don't you have to know how to do inventory in order to help?" Something was fishy.

Lil gave a mischievous smile that Marlina knew well. "Given that, I used to work here and all, I told her I'd stay and help her."

"Okay, I'll stay too," she said, not having anything to do for the rest of the afternoon. "It would be fun."

Lilian frowned, shaking her head. "Don't be silly. You're dressed to go out around town, not hang around a clothing store."

"*You* were supposed to show me around, remember? I can't go looking around by myself." She had the worst sense of direction, and she wasn't one to wander around without a plan. *Then again, I am turning over a new leaf and trying new things*; she reminded herself. "Actually, you're right. I think I will go look around."

"Awesome." Lilian turned to Gabriel. "Are you free? Maybe you could show her around."

And there it is. Pick out a new outfit, look all cute. Inventory my ass. It was all an excuse to ger her alone with Gabriel. She should've seen this coming a mile away, but Lil was very sneaky about this little plan of hers.

"Mia no longer needs my help, so I'd love to." Smiling, he held his hand out to her. "Would you accompany me to dinner?"

Is he kidding? I'll accompany his fine ass anywhere he wants. Though, thankfully, she didn't voice that thought. Nodding, she replied, "Sure, if you're not too busy."

"I know this quiet little café only locals go to, and the veranda is private."

Her cheeks grew warm, and her stomach somersaulted at the thought of being alone with him. Not to mention, the sexy look he was giving her. Somehow, he made those simple words sound so erotic.

Smiling, she took the hand he'd offered. "Sounds wonderful."

As he pulled her toward the door with him, his gaze stayed on her. There was something in his look that she couldn't quite decipher. Something that made her want to curl into his side and beg him to touch her everywhere. Goosebumps broke out across her flesh, and she shivered at the thought. She definitely wanted to see this man's naughty side. God, she knew she shouldn't want that, but she couldn't help it. The draw, the attraction, the fire…it was scorching. Despite the wise words screaming in her head, she kept being pulled to Gabriel like a moth to a flame.

"You know this cafe well?" As soon as she asked the question, a burn settled into her stomach, and her heart kicked heavily in her chest. A secluded café, he probably took a lot of women there. A romantic candlelight meal outside under the stars. Women ate up romantic gestures like that. Not that it should bother her; they were just friends. So, what was this ugly burn in the middle of her gut?

"I like the quiet atmosphere, and the food is good," he paused. "This isn't someplace I bring anyone."

"Oh," she said quickly, worried that she'd voiced her thoughts out loud without realizing it. "I didn't…I mean," she stammered.

"*Va bene*," he said, chuckling softly. "I just wanted you to know. This is a special place."

She ignored the excited up-kick of her heartbeat and her trembling hands. Smiling, she turned her attention to the scenery as they walked. The cobblestone street they walked down made her feel like she'd been transported back through time. Ivy grew up the stone and brick walls of buildings that looked like they had been built well over a century ago. Cast-iron balconies with decorative flowerpots and rolling clotheslines full of clothing added to the old world feel of things.

As they ventured farther along their path, they came to an older woman, who stood off to the side, by a brick wall, holding a large wicker basket filled with bright red roses. "*Un bel fiore, per una bella signora?*"

Stopping, Gabriel replied, "*Sì.*" Handing the woman a few coins for one of the roses, he turned, offering the beautiful, fragrant flower to Marlina. "A beautiful red rose, for *bella mia signora.*"

Blushing, she took the flower from him. She might not remember a whole lot of Italian, but she did understand that, *my beautiful lady*. It was the sweetest compliment she ever got.

"Thank you." Marlina smiled, lifting the rose to her nose and taking a deep breath of its fragrant aroma. She had to admit, it was damn hard not to be charmed by this man, and her guard fell a little more. She wasn't fooling herself. Maybe he wasn't being genuine, maybe he was like this with every woman that crossed his path. It didn't matter, she liked it. She was enjoying the attention, and the sweet words he spoke to her. It'd been a long time since a man said anything sweet or charming to her.

Continuing on their path, they came to an abrupt halt as two rambunctious boys ran in front of them. Nearby, Marlina took in the sight of a young couple sitting by a fountain kissing or taking pictures together while others threw coins into the water and made their wishes.

With all of the walking they were doing, Marlina was quite grateful for the shoes her sister had picked out for her. The beautiful peep-toe sandals with the small heel were much different than her usual, practical, and simple shoes. She loved them. They made her feel feminine and pretty.

As the street ended, so did their walk. From what Marlina could see, there was nothing in front of them but a brick wall with ivy crawling up the sides and a slew of windows stretching the length of it. Above them, an old lady sat out on her rocking chair, watching them.

"Did we pass it?" she asked, looking around for a sign or something.

"This is it," Gabriel said, motioning to the small, plain door to their right.

It looked like nothing more than a door leading into someone's home. Certainly not how she would expect a café door to look. The door was made from wood and appeared extremely solid, held firmly in place with cast iron hinges. The brick stoop leading up to the door was comprised of four beautifully curved steps.

"This is the place?" Marlina asked in confusion.

"*Si.*" Walking up the steps, he pushed open the door. "Welcome to *Giardino Nascosto,* the Hidden Garden. This little place might not seem like much from out here but wait until you see the inside." Pulling her to the door, he added, "And the food is *delizioso*."

Walking inside, she gasped, looking around the small cafe. Gabriel was certainly correct; it was absolutely breathtaking. The atmosphere was calming, giving patrons the feeling of being hidden away someplace where no one could reach you or bother you. She could literally feel the stress of the outside world melting away from her. The vibe was meditative and calming. "Amazing," she muttered.

As they ventured farther inside, Marlina found that there were several tables scattered around the main floor in no particular order. They were small, seating anywhere from one to four people, but there were several tables pushed together for larger groups. Candles in red, glass stained jars were at the center of each table, along with a bottle of Chianti.

Uneven stones made up the floor, reminding her of her grandmother's kitchen. In America, buildings were made out of wood and drywall, but not here in Italy. Here, every building was built from stone and brick. Old buildings that had been standing for hundreds of years were considered brand-new.

In this cafe, it was no different. Stone and brick everywhere you looked, from the walls to the beautiful arched doorways. Simple cast iron sconces hung on the walls, lit candles resting in their centers. The fixtures were used to create light, not decoration like back home. In truth, it took the darkness out of the place, creating a romantic glow in the room.

The bar across the back wall was a small, simple area with a counter full of various bottles of wine. There was nothing extravagant. The atmosphere was rustic and homey, sucking you in and making you feel instantly at ease and comfortable. Welcome.

"Wow," she muttered, following Gabriel through the main room. "You weren't lying. This place is amazing."

"Out here on the veranda is my favorite spot." Stepping to the side, he allowed her to walk out ahead of him. "What do you think?" he asked.

Somehow, the veranda was even more beautiful than the inside. Out here, it truly cut out the rest of the world. Behind the railing was a garden full of various types of flowers from roses, to orchids. At the back of the garden, a stone wall was completely covered in ivy. It grew everywhere here, it seemed. The calming sound of trickling water from the nearby fountain helped to soothe any anxiety one might have, melting it away into oblivion. Across the ceiling, twinkling lights stretched, hanging from the rafters, creating a romantic glow on the tables below.

Smiling, she stared at the fairy lights. "It's beautiful."

"Yes, it is," he replied. However, he wasn't looking at the lights, he was looking at her.

"You're not even looking," she said, motioning to the lights overhead.

With his gaze locked on her, he smiled, and inclined his head. "Yes, I am."

She felt heat rush to her cheeks. There is no way Gabriel was flirting with her. He was just being nice like old friends do but being here with Gabriel right now, the things he said, the way he looked at her, it felt freaking great. The thought had her stomach twisting in knots.

Pushing the thoughts from her mind, she followed as he led her over to a table in the far left-hand corner. Situated closest to the fountain, the table was beautiful. Hanging just over the railing, next to the table, was a beautiful purple orchid with white specks.

"I got this for you," he motioned to the orchid.

Marlina was stunned. He knew her favorite flower? "How did you know I loved orchids?"

Grinning, he pulled out her seat for her. "When I told you that I remembered everything about you. You don't think that included your favorite things?"

Gabriel carefully pushed the chair underneath her like a gentleman. Yet one more thing a man had never done for her. "I guess I just don't remember telling you very much about myself."

Sitting down opposite her, he flashed his panty-melting smile. "You told me enough." Looking to the waiter she hadn't even noticed approaching, Gabriel ordered something in Italian, and traded in the wine on the table for something else. Knowing him, and the fact he now ran a vineyard, the wine he requested was sure to be amazing.

"So, what did you order?" she asked.

"*Antipasto.*"

Damn, just the way he said it made her lady parts pulse. "Another favorite."

"Mine too." A few moments later, the waiter returned with a wine bottle. Turning the label toward Gabriel, he nodded. The waiter filled her glass first.

"What kind of wine is this?" Marlina wasn't familiar with too many wines, but this one smelled heavenly.

"It's an older Chianti." Picking up his glass, he swirled the wine and took a deep breath of the fresh aroma it released. "Outside of the vineyard, this is the only place that carries our Chianti from the earlier years when my father ran the vineyard. He always loved a great Chianti." Shaking his head, he took a sip of the velvety red liquid. "He might've been a bastard, but he knew the vines."

Not knowing what to say, she picked up her glass and took a drink. It was distinctive, with a slight hint of berry and a musty scent. The flavor was smoother and less smoky than she would've thought for a dry wine, which pleasantly surprised her.

Holding her wine glass, she cocked her head to the side as she studied him. He seemed to know so much about her; it was time she learned more about him.

Chapter 6

Gabriel tried to pay attention to what Marlina was talking about, but he kept getting lost in her captivating green eyes. She was so expressive, using her hands as she spoke, the animation on her face showing every bit of happiness and disappointment.

She wasn't the tall, glamorous type of woman he usually hooked up with. His usual type was looking for the same thing he was looking for—a night of hot sex, nothing more. Marlina was different, unique. She was a natural beauty, who didn't wear a pound of makeup, her tits weren't fake, and her ass was thick and luscious all on its own.

A lot of the women he'd dated over the years were extremely high maintenance. It wasn't something he'd minded; he understood the process of altering one's appearance to look a certain way. He'd done the same thing when he was younger.

As a youth, he was gangly, lean, and a bit on the nerdy side. He spent years lifting weights, and building up his endurance in an effort to sculpt his body to the way he wanted. His appearance had changed so much by the time he hit sixteen, girls were throwing themselves at him, and like any young man, he took advantage of it. When he turned eighteen, women, young and old, single and married, offered him no strings attached sex left and right. It seemed like every woman in town wanted a piece of him—every woman except Marlina.

Marlina didn't giggle or fall all over herself to get his attention. She wouldn't wear short skirts and low-cut blouses, hoping he'd look her way. But she would watch him. He'd caught her a few times. She'd quickly look away, of course, trying not to get caught, but he always saw the way her cheeks pinkened. Even then, the women he was used to never blushed. They weren't shy about anything. He liked the fact that Marlina could be embarrassed. It was refreshing, and it turned him on a lot.

After their kiss among the grapes that summer afternoon, he'd been hoping to do more than kiss later that night, a horny teenage boy and all that. It never happened. Marlina's mother took her back to America the next morning. He waited, hoping to see her again, but that too never happened. He tried to track her down but looking for someone in New York City was like looking for a needle in a haystack. Still, he tried. Hell, did he try.

Gabriel knew Marlina's mother was controlling and manipulative. She was determined to keep Marlina away from him and anyone else she deemed a threat. From what information he'd been able to get from Lilian, their mother was monitoring any form of communication Marlina had. It was all a manipulation tactic to gain control over her daughters. Lilian wasn't buying it but Marlina buckled, not that he could blame her. It was hard to resist a parent. Eventually, he learned Marlina married a man her mother approved of and Gabriel was crushed. He lost any hope of ever seeing her again.

Gabriel was certain Marlina was and had always been his destiny. They had to separate for a time, but she was back now. He wasn't sure how long she would stay, but he was going to do his best to convince her Italy was her new home.

Thinking about Marlina and her marriage, he couldn't help but wonder what sort of man was stupid enough to let a rare gem such as Marlina get away. Not that he wasn't happy that her dumbass husband let her go. The way he saw it, her ex's loss was his gain. There was something that kept nagging at him; he noticed a couple of things that made him wonder about exactly how her ex treated her. Little things that he picked up on because he paid such close attention to her, shaking her head in denial when he complimented her though she didn't say anything vocally to deny it, and the way she seemed to shy away when a man smiled at her. There were many, he paid attention. She didn't, and when she did, she'd act like she saw nothing, just looking away and busying herself with something else. He was very interested to finding out what those things were all about, but he also knew that now wasn't the time to ask personal questions.

There were many times over the years that he wondered about the woman she'd grown into, how beautiful she turned out, and wished he was there to see it. He would imagine, but his imagination paled in comparison to the sexy woman sitting on the other side of the table from him. His gaze roamed over her beautiful body, eyeing the neckline of her dress, which dropped low enough to showcase her large, supple breasts. Gaze lowering, he sucked in a sharp breath at the sight of her puckered nipples pressing against the tight material of her dress. He imagined pushing down the neckline of her dress until her perfect peaks came into view, allowing him to skim his teeth over those hard nipples before sucking them into his mouth. His cock twitched, and he shifted in his seat, forcing himself to get a grip.

"Gabriel? Gabriel?" Marlina said, snapping her fingers in front of his face.

He jerked his attention back to her face. "*Si cosa?*"

She laughed. "Did you hear anything I just said?"

Laughing to himself, he shook his head and reached across the table to take her hand in his. "*Mi dispiace*," he apologized. "No."

Smirking, she narrowed her eyes slightly but didn't pull her hand from his. "No?"

He shook his head, running the callused pad of his thumb back and forth over her knuckles. "I got lost in my thoughts."

Still smiling, she just shook her head. "I'm curious about the tattoo across your knuckle."

Tightening his hand into a fist, he raised it up slightly. "I got it when I was twenty-five."

"Any particular reason?"

He nods. "To remind me to not only stay true to myself," his gaze, full of heat, locked with hers. "And to stay true to those I care about."

"Wow," she muttered. "An important tattoo."

He nodded. "*Sì*."

"What were you thinking when I was rambling nonsense just a few seconds ago?"

"I was thinking about the last summer I saw you," he admitted.

She didn't look at him, only stared down at her plate, and attempted to pull her hand from his. "It was a beautiful summer," she said in a low voice.

Tightening his grip on her hand, he held it firmly, letting her know that he wasn't letting her go anywhere. "Our first kiss." He kept his voice low and seductive, knowing he'd get her attention.

Her gaze jerked up to his, and he grinned. "W-what?" she stammered as red spread up her neck and across her cheeks.

She was embarrassed. *Interesting*. He liked it. "Our first kiss," he repeated.

"Our only kiss," she offered with a nervous chuckle.

He shook his head, lifting her hand to his mouth. "No, I don't think so," he muttered, stretching out her fingers but still holding her hand firmly.

She nodded. "It was."

"Maybe back then." Lowering his head, he kept his gaze locked on her and brushed his lips across the tips of her fingers. "I intend for there to be many more in our future." Gabriel watched as her chest rose and fell more rapidly, her pupils dilating. Oh yeah, she wanted him. She was just unsure of herself.

"You do?" Shock laced her words.

Seductively, he sucked the tip of her index finger into his mouth. Lust hit his gut hard, pants tightening as his cock hardened. Fuck, he wanted her. Keeping his gaze locked with hers, he wrapped his tongue around the slender digit, flicking the tip of his tongue across the soft pad before slipping the digit slowly out of his mouth.

"Many more," he whispered.

Taking a deep, shaky breath, she glanced away from him and cleared her throat. "Gabriel," she said, bringing her gaze back to his, "are you trying to seduce me?"

He laughed. She had more nerve than she thought, and it pleased him. Hmm, just thinking about her extremes of shy and audacious behavior turned him on more than he thought possible. It also meant he needed to step up his little dance of seduction. "Do you want me to seduce you?"

Laughing, she pulled her hand from his grasp. "Maybe that's a question best answered at a later date."

Just then, the waiter returned with the appetizers he'd ordered. He could've kicked the guy. Of all the times to be interrupted it, had to be right then when she was finally flirting back with him. Instead of getting angry, he decided to take it as a win. Anticipation could go a long way in building the sexual tension between them.

"*Grazie*," he told the waiter as he began to plate their appetizers. Gabriel stared at her as he laid his napkin across his lap. She smiled brightly up at the waiter as he placed some cheese, prosciutto, and tomatoes drizzled with olive oil onto the small serving plate in front of her.

He couldn't help but smile as he watched the man soak up the attention Marlina was giving him. She was completely oblivious to the power her beauty held over men. Gabriel was pretty sure the man offered to bring her a taste of the house specials to help her decide what she preferred for dinner just to get her to beam up at him in thanks one more time. Many women he'd been acquainted with over the years could do the same thing, but they all knew they were doing it. Marlina's reaction was so endearing because it was sweet and innocent, honest. It was the reason they were all tripping over themselves to help her and eating out of her hand.

The girl he'd known grew into a beautiful woman who was a contradiction on every level, and that intrigued him. He was determined to have her, not just for a night but for forever. She may be leery, but he was a patient man with more than his fair share of seduction knowledge. In the end, he always got what he wanted and what he wanted was Marlina.

Walking slowly by the pond behind her grandmother's house, Marlina couldn't stop smiling. It was the most pleasant and surprising afternoon that she ever had. It was yet another thing that made her look back at her marriage and cringe. Not once did she ever feel like she felt right now, glowing inside and out from the afternoon spent with Gabriel and all his charm totally focused on her. It felt good. Better than good, it was amazing. There was so much neglect in her relationship with Adam. If she were honest with herself, she'd have to say it was on both sides. Adam didn't try to get close to her, to love her, but she couldn't say she tried either. What did that say about them?

Why hadn't she realized any of this before? She never saw it before, but she was seeing it now and what was beginning to take shape was that maybe she wasn't the only one trying to pretend that her marriage was a happy one.

"Thank you for allowing me to take you to dinner," Gabriel's deep voice broke into her thoughts.

Smiling brightly, she clasped her hands in front of her. "I had a great time." Watching him out of the corner of her eye, she tried to gauge what he was thinking. His attention was focused on the pond and the silvery moonlight reflecting off the dark, rippling surface of the water. A beautiful weeping willow tree with long, immaculately trimmed branches grew nearby. A white bistro-style table with four chairs rested under the sagging branches.

This pond was her special place. When she spent summers here, she would spend a lot of her time relaxing in the grass here, reading, drawing, or painting. Things that made her happy that she wasn't allowed to do at home. Back with her mother, all she ever did was study and have lessons of every kind. Dance, ballet, music, tennis, every lesson that her mother could think of that would indicate that she was of good stock from good breeding. Made her sound like a damn horse, and it's pretty much how her mother made her feel. Vivian wasn't big on attention, sentiment, or being a mother for that matter. She was more like a PR business manager, always planning for her image, her future, and never asking her input on it. No wonder she looked forward to her time here and never wanted it to end.

The other night she came out here with a book and a nice glass of wine. The lamp she brought was old fashioned, and the flickering flame cast a golden glow over the table, and that, coupled with the serene pond, made her feel like she was in a painting. It relaxed her and made her mind wander. Unfortunately, where it wandered to was her past and what occurred over the years. There was nothing in her memories of what she wanted to do or anything she had chosen for herself. Everything was meticulously planned out by her mother, right down to the man she married.

"You love this pond, si?" Gabriel asked, giving her a much-needed reprieve from her thoughts.

"Yeah, I love coming down here to read or think." She took a deep breath, drawing the fresh air into her lungs and feeling peace set into her soul as her previous thoughts melted away.

"What do you think about?" Gabriel asked softly.

She shrugged. "My life back in America, and how empty I let it get." His warm palm slid against hers, the calluses scratching across her soft skin and making her body prickle with sensual awareness.

He laced their fingers together. "It happens," he muttered, pulling her toward the weeping willow tree. Just past the table and chairs was a blanket and lantern set up under the shelter of its branches. Sitting on the blanket was a bottle of *Sassicaia* and two crystal wine glasses.

"How did you do this?" Marlina asked in shock.

Pleased by her reaction, he chuckled and pulled her toward the blanket. "I must confess, I had inside help."

"Lilian?" She wasn't really surprised, no one could keep a secret like her sister.

He nodded. "I hope you don't mind."

Was Lilian behind everything? She wondered. Is she the one who suggested dinner and an evening under the stars with a bottle of wine? Is he only doing all of this because of a push from her sister? Or was all this his idea with some help from her sister? She was having such a good time, she wasn't sure she wanted to know the answer to any of that. But she had to ask.

"Did my sister put you up to all of this?" She nearly choked on the words.

His head snapped in her direction. "What?" he asked, eyes narrowing slightly.

The intensity in his gaze took her by surprise. Trying to pull her hand from his, she swallowed hard. "I was just wondering if Lilian set any of this up. You know, the store, dinner." She made a sweeping motion with her arm. "This."

Gabriel moved so fast she didn't have time to react. Cupping her face with both hands, he captured her mouth with his in one fiery kiss. A gasp of surprise slipped from her. He took full advantage, slipping his tongue past her lips and into her mouth.

Moaning, her eyes closed, and she melted against him as she soaked up the spicy, minty taste of him. His lips were warm and wet, soft and firm as he took control of the kiss in a way that she never experienced before. Gabriel didn't coax, he demanded. Timidly, her tongue dipped past his lips and into his mouth, brushing up against his. He tasted good.

A deep groan tore from his throat as his hand left her cheek to cup her nape, holding her still as he tilted his head, deepening the kiss. Excitement surged through her as his other hand drifted down her back, toward her waist. Resting his hand on her hip for a moment, he slid his arm around her waist and drew her body against his.

Moving of their own accord, she ran her hands up his bulging biceps, across his shoulders, and wrapped them around his neck. Rising on her tiptoes, she opened her mouth wider, allowing him to kiss her deeper and with more passion. Thank god her body was pressed firmly against his because her knees felt like jelly. The only thing keeping her on her feet was the strong arm wrapped tightly around her waist. Her fingers pressed into his hard muscles as a delicious fog seeped over her mind making it impossible for her to think of anything but the feel and taste of him.

Gabriel groaned again, louder, sending a surge of moisture flooding between her thighs. Her nipples tightened. She whimpered as the sensitive peaks scratched against the lacy material of her bra. Marlina was so turned on she tried to press her thighs together to get some desperately needed relief. All she wanted to do was rip Gabriel's clothes off and rub her naked body all over him.

The press of his lips grew softer, as he slowly withdrew his delicious tongue and brought the mind-blowing kiss to an end. His lips left her hers, moving up and dragging his lips in light kisses across her cheek until he reached her ear.

"Did that feel like your sister's idea?" he whispered, his warm breath drifting over her skin.

"Gabriel," she gasped, pleasure shooting through her like a bullet.

"Answer me," he demanded, sucking her earlobe into his mouth and skimming his teeth across the delicate flesh just hard enough to make her shiver.

"I can't think," she moaned as his lips traveled down her neck, across her collarbone to her shoulder.

His erotic whisper sent more chills sweeping through her. "First thing that comes to your mind."

"I've never been kissed like that," she admitted.

Leaning back, a deep frown crinkled his brow as he stared into her eyes. "What?"

"I've never had a kiss like that." Her chin dropped. and she stared at the ground, the way she always did when she made an embarrassing confession. Spilling the less than erotic secrets of her and Adam's loveless marriage would just kill the mood, and that was something she really didn't want to do.

"Marlina—" Gabriel coaxed.

Pulling away from him, she prevented him from finishing his sentence. Pushing away the burgeoning emotions, she pulled her humor around her like a protective shield. "I've got an idea. Instead of sitting out here, why don't we go for a walk?"

Cocking his head, he stared at her, a pensive look on his handsome face. "Where to?"

"The vineyard." She held her hand out to him. She used to walk through the vines at night with Mia. It would be so nice to relive some of those memories. They're some of the happiest of her childhood."

Taking her hand in his, he pulled her a step closer. "Marlina…"

"Please?" she begged, interrupting him as she poked out her bottom lip, hoping to change his mind.

With an exaggerated sigh, he tilted his head back briefly before caving. "Okay, fine." Focusing his attention back on her, a serious expression crossed his face. "But when this walk is over, we talk about this."

"Talk about what?" she asked, feigning innocence as her heart pounded in dread. He wasn't going to let it go, and she knew it.

"Lina," he warned.

"Fine," she huffed. "We'll talk about it later." Like hell, they would, not if she could help it. She never should've brought the damn thing up, and if her brain hadn't been fried by the amazing kiss he'd given her, she would've had all her brain cells and wouldn't have said anything. She'd have to think of another way to distract him and keep him from remembering what he wanted to talk about.

TUSCAN HEAT

Chapter 7

Gabriel wasn't stupid. There was something Marlina was keeping from him. Something bad, and he was willing to bet it had everything to do with her piece of shit ex-husband. She seemed relaxed as she walked through the rows of vines with him, but he knew better. He noticed the tension in her shoulders and how rigid she held her back as they walked. There was a story here, and he was determined to find out what it was.

"So, is it like you remember?" he asked softly. Since she was so reluctant to talk about her situation, he wanted to keep the mood light in hopes of getting her to feel comfortable again.

It worked. She smiled, and her shoulders relaxed. The full moon poured its silvery light down over the endless rows of vines. In this darkness, with the light pouring down, there was a majestic feeling almost like you were stepping into a painting. She would love it, women always did.

Shifting his stance, he took a deep breath, uncomfortable with the direction of his thoughts. He'd brought a lot of women here in the past—mainly because it was an excellent seduction tool. It always loosened them up and made them feel all dreamy. Gabriel found that when they were intoxicated, not by alcohol, but by the beauty of the scenery, they were feeling all romantic and also horny. There was no other way to put it. A man used everything he could when trying to impress a woman and get her into bed. It was just one of those things.

Even though it was a tool he used often, it's not what he was trying with Marlina. He hadn't wanted to bring her here, among the vines where he brought so many other women. He'd wanted that picnic under the stars, to talk and to kiss, then to see where things went from there. He'd wanted her for what seemed like forever, but he didn't want to rush things. He didn't want it to be like all the other women he'd spent time with. She was different.

"Yes," she said with a sigh. "I'd forgotten how beautiful it was."

He watched as the gentle breeze blew strands of her dark hair into her face. Out here in the moonlight, she looked ethereal. "So, had I," he muttered in agreement. However, he wasn't talking about the scenery.

She laughed, looking at him. "How could you have forgotten? You live here. You see it every day."

"True. You know I always knew I wanted to be here," he said, changing the subject. Taking her hand in his, he walked down the path zigzagging through the vines. "Even as a child, I wanted to do what my father and my grandfather did. After my parents divorced, I could legally take over running the vineyard, but I was only eighteen, and my mother wouldn't hear of it."

"Why not?" She asked, genuinely interested, which was something unusual to him. The women he'd been here with acted interested in what he had to say but, in reality, were far from it.

He shrugged. "She wanted Lucien and I to have other options, not locked into one thing. We did, thanks to her. Lucien found his niche in finance. Not surprising considering numbers were always his thing and planning. Me, my heart has always been here," he explained, motioning to the vineyard. "After I had my experiences, explored a few options, I came back home knowing this was the place I wanted to be. Home isn't home just because of the memories from your childhood, or because it's a place you can return to when you need to get on your feet. It's a feeling in here," he said, pressing her hand to his hard chest, right over his heart. He longed to feel her touch on his bare skin, but it wasn't the right time.

Spreading her fingers out, it felt as if she tried to touch as much of him as she could. "You're right," she whispered. "It's beautiful."

Cupping her cheek, he took a step closer to her. "I wasn't talking about the vineyard."

He watched her throat work as she swallowed. "Oh." Looking up at him, eyes wide and blazing with rekindled desire, she hesitated. "What were you talking about?"

Chuckling, he bent his head down and pressed a kiss to her bare shoulder. "You." He knew he shouldn't be kissing her, but he was powerless to stop himself.

Tilting her head, she gave him better access to her neck. "Gabriel," she moaned breathlessly. Grasping the material of his shirt in both hands, she pulled him closer.

Kissing his way to her ear, he nipped her skin along the way. "*Sí.*" Flicking her earlobe with the tip of his tongue, he sucked it into his mouth before biting down gently.

Her body jerked as she let out a gasp. "Oh God, that feels good."

Wrapping his arms around her waist, he pulled her against him, groaning at the feel of her soft curves molding to the hard planes of his body. Every good intention he had fled his mind. Raw, hot need seized him, leaving him unable to think of anything but the taste and feel of her.

Gently brushing her lips across his cheek, she whispered in his ear. "I want you to kiss me again."

Closing his eyes, he tried desperately to hold onto his self-control. Sadly, he lost the battle when she sucked his bottom lip into her mouth and bit down gently before letting the plump flesh slide out between her teeth.

Losing his grip on his control, he captured her lips with a desperation he hadn't felt in a long time, if ever. Desire pounded in his head, lust shooting to his cock and making him painfully hard. She was here in his arms, and she wanted him to take her. Maybe she didn't say it with words, but she didn't have to; her body spoke for her.

He could have her, take her right here and now. He wanted her more than he wanted his next breath, but it wasn't right. After the way she'd reacted back at the pond, he couldn't help but feel like he was taking advantage of her. When Gabriel made love to her, he wanted to know she was as mad for him as he was for her. Not because she was running away from the past.

With that thought nagging at him, he knew he had to stop things before they got out of hand, before he wasn't able to resist.

I just need another taste of her. Just a little more, and then I'll stop, he told himself. It was going to be a difficult to keep that vow.

Marlina was lost in a euphoric, sexual haze that prevented her from thinking about anything other than the feel of Gabriel's body pressed against her and his incredibly skilled mouth as he kissed his way across her skin. She'd always thought it was ridiculous when she'd read about women melting in a man's embrace. She was positive such a thing had to be exaggerated. It wasn't.

In Gabriel's strong embrace, pressed against his muscular body, her bones turned to jelly. She clung to him, knowing the only thing that kept her on her feet was his strong arm wrapped around her waist. He seemed to surround her, enveloping every inch of her, and the only thing that existed at this moment was him, his taste, smell, and his touch.

As another soft moan escaped her lips, it sounded more like a purr to her ears, but she couldn't bring herself to care. He felt so good and tasted even better. Breaking the kiss, Gabriel dragged his lips across her cheek to her neck. Needing him closer, she tilted her head to the side. Thankfully, he got the hint.

Trailing kisses down her neck and back up again, he left a blazing trail of fire everywhere his lips touched. As his hands slid to her waist, she circled her hips, desperate to feel him against her aching center.

"I want you," she whispered, trailing her hand from his shoulder and down his chest before grasping his hard cock through his slacks. Desire, sharp and vivid, flashed through her so strongly she trembled from the force of it.

"Marlina," Gabriel whispered as his head fell back and he let out a deep, masculine groan.

The metal clanking of his belt sounded in the silence as her hands trembled as she began unbuckling it. She wanted to see him, feel him, taste him.

Head snapping down, his eyes flew open just as her fingertips brushed his hot flesh. Grunting, he thrust himself into her palm, her fingers trailing up and down his hard length. He was so hard, so hot. God she couldn't wait to taste him, to feel him thrusting his hard length deep inside her.

"Gabriel," she whispered. "Make love to me." Grabbing his hand, she guided it between her thighs. His calloused fingertips brushed over the smooth flesh of her inner thigh. Heat shot through her veins like electricity, lighting up all her erogenous zones in one brutal hit. Widening her stance, she urged him without words to continue his exploration. "Right here, right now. Please," she begged.

"Marlina," Gabriel rasped, cupping her face and staring into her eyes. Brushing his thumb back and forth over her cheekbone, he drew in a deep breath and spoke. "We can't."

Staring at him, she swallowed hard, a frown creasing her brow. "Why?"

Lowering his hands, he rested them on his hips, head lowered, gaze firmly focused on her. "Not like this," he whispered. Taking a deep breath, he said, "I think we should go back."

"Not like this? Or not like me?" Tears threatened to fall. She managed to choke them back. Hurt and humiliation burned in her gut. Maybe he didn't say those words directly, but he didn't have to. What man turned down a woman offering sex if he wanted her? He probably had tons of women to choose from. There was probably one waiting at home for him right now. Here she was trying to seduce him and failing miserably. How could she have gotten everything so wrong? "I'm sorry," she apologized, immediately turning, and heading back the way they came.

"Marlina, wait." He grabbed her arm gently.

"No." Jerking her arm from his hand, she spat, "It's fine."

"Stop." Anger laced his command.

Despite herself, she froze at the authority in his voice, and looked at him from over her shoulder.

A muscle twitched along his jaw as he stepped closer to her. She didn't turn around. "Will you at least let me explain? I—"

"There's nothing to explain," she said, cutting him off. "I had a wonderful evening. Thank you for showing me around and taking me to dinner." She tried to smile but failed miserably. "I know my way back," she said, continuing to walk again, nearly tripping in her hurry to get away from him.

"Marlina, wait."

She heard footsteps behind her and picked up the pace. The last thing she wanted was for him to catch her. The evening had turned into a pathetic mess, and the ice cream on top of the shit cake would be him seeing the tears streaming down her cheeks.

"Don't follow me." She was close to begging him to just stay away from her. "Just leave me alone."

He obeyed her wishes and stayed back. Thank god for small favors.

She couldn't believe how big a fool she made of herself. Gabriel was a handsome, passionate, sexy man, and he didn't want her. Why would he, when he could literally have any woman he set his sights on?

'You're just not the type of woman that drives a man crazy.' Adam's words echoed in her head like a broken record. No matter how many times she tried to push him and the things he said away, there they were creeping up. Making her doubt herself. Now tonight, with what just happened, it lent power to all the shit Adam said to her over the years. If a man really wanted a woman, he wouldn't just turn her down, would he? It didn't make any sense to her.

If Adam didn't want her, he should've just told her. She would understand. He didn't have to play the role of interested, doting lover just to humiliate her.

What an asshole.

This would be the first and last time he made a fool out of her.

TUSCAN HEAT

Chapter 8

"Why?" Lilian asked, folding her arms over her chest.

"Because I don't want to talk about it." Patting her face dry, Marlina took extra time on her eyes so she could hold off on looking at her irritating sister for a moment longer.

"You never want to talk about anything. So, what else is new?" Walking over to Marlina, Lil ripped the towel away from her, grabbed her other hand, and led her to her bed. "Here," she said, handing her a full glass of red wine.

"Really?" Marlina arched a brow. "It's ten in the morning."

Lilian shrugged. "You can eat some pancakes afterward, soak it up." Lil tapped her leg, drawing Marlina's attention back to her. "Now, I'm not leaving here until you tell me what happened."

"You're such a pain in the ass," she sighed, taking a large gulp of the red wine. It was good, but it did nothing to push back the memories from last night or even ease the sting from Gabriel's rejection. "At first, he brought me back by the pond for the picnic you helped him set up. I wanted to take a walk in the vineyard. It was so beautiful, the smell in the air, the silvery moonlight—all of it. Well, we talked, and one thing led to another. Next thing you know, we were making-out right there, in nature, under the stars. It was so romantic or would've been." She swallowed hard from the embarrassment and humiliation of the entire situation.

Lilian frowned. "Would've been?"

"And exactly what I said." Sighing heavily, she dropped her head into her hands. "I got carried away and asked him to...to..." she shook her head, closing her eyes tightly. God, she couldn't even say it.

"Do what?" Lilian asked, tilting her head to the side. "Fuck you?"

Marlina glared at her sister. "No, he wouldn't do my taxes," she said sarcastically. "What do you think?"

"What happened?"

She shrugged. "I don't know. He just stopped."

Lilian arched a brow. "Stopped?"

"Are you a parrot?" She asked, exasperated. "He didn't want to do it. Said we shouldn't." Standing up, she downed the rest of her wine and waved her hand. "He said some other stuff, but I stopped listening after the humiliating burn of the first rejection. Plus, it was hard to hear anything over the roaring in my ears."

"Wow. Did he give a reason?"

"Not really." Her heart clenched, and her stomach flip-flopped. "He said, not like this or something."

"Wait. So, he didn't say no? He said, not now?"

"Jeeze, Lil, do we have to do a postmortem?" Marlina groaned, looking around the room for the wine bottle. "I need to forget anything ever happened and just go back to my lonely, pathetic life." She grabbed the bottle from next to Lilian.

Lilian snatched it back from her. "You're not going to solve this problem by getting drunk at 10AM!"

"It's five o'clock somewhere." Lina reached for the bottle, but her sister held it just out of reach.

"Drowning your sorrows in a bottle of wine before noon might not be the best way to deal with your emotions."

"What?" She was seriously getting a headache from all of this back and forth. "You were the one to offer me a glass of wine, if you recall."

"I offered a glass, not a bottle," Lilian corrected.

"What's the difference?"

Pretending to think about it for a moment, she finally spoke. "Hmmm—how about lucidity?"

"How about I don't give a shit?" she snapped. "Give me the damn bottle."

Walking over to the balcony, Lilian looked over her shoulder. "No." Without another word, she poured the bottle out the railing.

She shook her head. "You're mental, do you know that?"

"Thank you." Lil paused, drawing in a deep breath. "Now, tell me exactly what he said."

"He just said he didn't want it to be like that?"

Lilian rubbed her chin, genuinely confused. "Like what?"

Marlina lowered her head in embarrassment. "In the vineyard, I guess." Her chin trembled as she spoke. "Or maybe he meant like me. I don't know. I don't plan on finding him so he can clarify anything, thank you very much."

"Don't be so dense," Lilian shot back.

"Excuse me?" She knew her sister was blunt, sometimes hurtfully so, but she'd been expecting some compassion with this.

"Did it ever occur to you that maybe he didn't want JUST a quick fuck outside, on the ground, surrounded by grapes?"

She rolled her eyes at the same time. "What man isn't hoping for one?"

"A man who really cares about the woman he's trying to hook up with."

"Trying to hook up with? Do you hear yourself?" She snorted. "That argument is points for my side because you're actually trying to tell me he passed up having sex with me because he cares about me. How in the hell does that make any sense at all?"

Lilian nodded. "Make sense or not, that's exactly what I'm telling you."

Instead of making Marlina feeling better, Lil's suggestion made her feel worse, and even more embarrassed. She didn't think it was possible, but apparently, it was. Was Lil right? She couldn't be. Could she? "It doesn't matter. Whatever his reason, it's too much. Embarrassment and rejection like that maims you."

"So, you're going to avoid him for what, forever?" Lilian asked.

"That's the plan. Just because I'm friends with his sister doesn't mean I have to see him." Marlina didn't care what her sister said There was no way she was feeling that mortification all over again.

"Fine, if that's the way you want it." Walking toward the door, Lilian muttered, "I knew this was going to happen."

"What?" Marlina shot back, curious as to what her sister was talking about.

Waving her hands in dismissal, Lil turned towards her sister. "This running thing."

"Running thing?" She asked in a monotone voice, totally confused.

"Yeah. Running. It's what you do."

"I'm not running." Marlina flinched at the accusation, maybe because deep down she knew that's exactly what she was doing.

"Yes, you are. You're scrutinizing every little thing that Gabriel is doing and comparing it to Adam. You think it's going to keep you from getting hurt, but it will keep you from experiencing what a good man, one who really likes you, has to offer you. If you don't get over what Adam did to you, and take a chance on love, you're going to stay locked in that marriage with him for the rest of your life. Is that what you want?"

Marlina couldn't believe what she was hearing, from Lilian no less. "Who in the hell are you to be lecturing me about getting over the past?" She demanded. "I mean, look to thy own ass first, right?"

"What the hell does that mean?" Lil questioned.

"You know exactly what it means. How many men have you given a chance to, an actual chance Lil, with no preconceived notions pushing you in one direction? How long has a relationship lasted for you since John walked away from you when you were pregnant with Rebekah?"

"This isn't about me," Lilian stated defensively.

"Of course not, because it never is. Your sexual practices are your own business, right? But you can tell me everything you think about my situation and just shut down when I bring up things, you're too afraid to face."

"I'm not afraid."

"Of course, you are. It's why you can't look past the shortcomings of your own intimacy issues."

"I don't have relationship issues." Lilian countered, folding her arms over her chest. "I haven't been a monk, you know."

"I'm not talking about sex, Lil," she sighed. "I'm talking about emotion, a connection, a feeling, you know, something that lasts longer than an orgasm."

Lilian opened her mouth to say something, but then shut it. Clenching her jaw, her nostrils flared. "You know, this isn't about me. The men I go out with aren't looking past much more than I am. You, on the other hand, have a real chance at a genuinely good man here." Walking to the door, she turned slightly to look at Marlina. "And you're just going to throw it all away because you're fucking scared." Grabbing the doorknob, she opened the door and walked out, slamming it behind her.

Taking a deep breath, Marlina released it slowly as she turned from the door, running her fingers through her hair. Lilian was right, and she knew it. She was afraid to get close to Gabriel because of what happened in her marriage. Adam had liked her in the beginning, at least she thought he had, but then suddenly he stopped, and that's what she was really afraid of. Giving love and relationship another try, only to have the man change his mind. No explanation, no warning, just nothing anymore. Fuck, she couldn't think. She was so damn confused about everything. Gabriel, Adam, her marriage, her past, fucking everything.

Maybe Lilian was right. Maybe she was more afraid than she realized. This whole thing with Gabriel was turning out to be a bigger risk than she was willing to take, maybe. God, Marlina wished she knew what she was feeling or had a fortune teller nearby. Maybe they could tell her what to do, what path she should take that wouldn't lead to a destructive future.

Was it asking too much for things in her life, just once, to be easy?

Marlina sat by the water's edge, digging her toes into the soil, while spinning a rose petal back and forth between her thumb and middle finger. It was a beautiful day, not a single cloud in the sky. The sun shone through the branches of the tree behind her, golden rays cascading over her body. Everything around her seemed so cheerful, and she wished she was in the mood to enjoy such a lovely day, but she just wasn't feeling it.

Closing her eyes, she desperately tried to forget everything that happened last night, but no matter how hard she tried, it still played over and over in her head. Well, that and the fight with her sister. They both spoke the truth but unlike Lilian, Marlina used the truth to hurt her sister because, well, the truth hurt. Now, she's feeling pretty damn guilty over it. She needed to apologize. One more thing to the damn list of fucked up things.

Maybe we can make up tonight over Biscotti and coffee, she wondered to herself. It was a good plan as long as Lilian didn't want to hash out her feelings about Gabriel again.

"*Ciao.*" The painfully familiar deep voice sends a chill rolling down her spine. The seductive, masculine voice had goosebumps breaking out across her skin. "Damn it, Lilian," she muttered under her breath. Even though the irritation at her sister, she was glad her sister never listened to her. This was forcing Marlina to set the record straight between her and Gabriel. Granted, it might have been something she was running from, but she had to admit, she needed it.

"We need to talk," Gabriel said, coming around to stand next to her. "I––"

Rising to her feet, she kept her gaze on anything but him. "There's really no need." Smiling the detached, fake smile she'd perfected over the years, she added, "Let's just forget last night ever happened, okay?"

"Forget?" There was an edge to his voice.

"Yeah." She cleared her throat, her gaze shooting to his face. "I think it's for the best."

His ordinarily light gray eyes that sparkled with charming mischief were now dark and stormy. Along his strong jaw, a muscle pulsed, effectively turning her on, despite her resolve to stay indifferent to him. Her gaze darted away from him. *Shit, even with anger pouring off of him, he is still so incredibly hot. There is something deeply wrong with me;* maybe she needed to seek out some therapy or something.

"Is that so?" he asked, narrowing his eyes.

Clearing her throat, she nodded. "Yes, and pick back up as friends," she stressed.

Glaring, he stepped closer to her. "*Amici? Cazzo essere amici,*" he growled.

"I don't want to be your friend."

Those words shocked her. Why was he so upset? She was the rejected one, mortified and having to face him again. Here she was extending an olive branch, and he was being a dick. "I don't know why you're so angry, but I can understand the situation."

Taking a deep breath, he blew it out slowly. "And what exactly do you think you understand?"

She looked at the ground wishing this whole ordeal was over. Last night she'd lost her head. It wasn't her fault, though; the man could seriously kiss. He could probably melt the panties off a nun. "You're not attracted to me," she said, wincing at her own words. "I—" any further explanation was cut off by the firm pressure of his soft, warm lips pressed against hers.

Pulling back slightly, a startled gasp escaped her. Not wasting a second, Gabriel took full advantage, pushing his tongue past her parted lips. Damn, the man tasted good. Moaning, her hands glided over his solid pecs and his defined shoulders, winding around his strong neck. Slipping her fingers into his soft brown hair at the back of his neck, she moaned against his lips. Tilting her head to the side, she let him take the kiss deeper.

A loud groan rumbled from deep in his chest, as his strong arms wrapped around her like two steel bands, drawing her closer to him. Every inch of the man was rock hard, and it made her feel soft and delicate in his arms. Sighing, she melted against him, her soft curves cradling all his hard angles. They fit together perfectly, almost as if they were made for one another. She shook the thought away, which wasn't too difficult with Gabriel kissing her in such a passionate, delicious way. Hopeless romantic really wasn't her style, but her mind wandered to all kinds of scenarios, and they all involved her and Gabriel living happily ever after.

Gabriel's large hand slowly slid down her back, over her ass. Cupping her firm, round cheek, he brought her hips securely against his. Bringing his other hand up, he cupped the back of her neck, allowing him even more control over the kiss. It was a dominant move and turned her on in ways she never anticipated. Feeling the hard, hot press of his cock through his jeans and the thin material of her dress, she whimpered. Her body trembled uncontrollably with the lust surging through her system. She never felt anything close to the passion and heat she was experiencing right now just by being in Gabriel's arms with his lips pressed to hers.

Keeping his hands in place, he slowly brought the kiss to an end. A couple of soft, chaste presses, and he was pulling back from her. With eyes still closed, she swayed toward him, desperate for another taste.

He chuckled, brushing his thumb over her cheek. "Open your eyes," he murmured.

Doing as she'd been told, she looked up and met those amazing gray eyes of his. "Wow," she whispered. Her brain totally fried.

"*Bella mia,* did that feel like I don't want you?" His deep voice vibrated through her.

"No," she said, smiling. "It doesn't."

He bent his head to her ear. "Come with me," he whispered.

Breath catching in her throat, her heart rate kicked up. Her body clenched with need, stomach flipping in anticipation of what was going to happen next. She wasn't stupid. She knew what would happen if she went with him. Was she ready for that? Staring up into his stormy gray eyes, she licked her lips, moaning softly at the lingering taste of him there. He tasted of dark chocolate, sinful desires, and wicked hot pleasure. Oh yeah, she was so ready for this.

"O–okay," she said softly.

The desire in his eyes grew darker, hotter. "*Sí?*"

Giving a small smile, she nodded. "Yes."

Clenching his jaw, he stared down at her. "You know what I'm asking," he said, voice hoarse. The intense look in his eyes had heat curling through her veins, making every cell in her body quiver. Breathless and light-headed was a strange combination when you were trying to think straight and something she'd never quite felt before, not to this extreme. Her hands were pressed against his chest, just over his heart, and she hoped he didn't feel the trembling ripple through her entire body. His heart was racing just as fast as hers.

Insecurity swirled in her gut. Trying to spread and make her second guess herself. Negative thoughts tried to push through her brain, pushing out the happiness and excitement she was feeling. Adam loved to remind her of just how much she was lacking. One thing she learned since coming to Italy and seeing the appreciative looks and whistles she got from random men was that Adam was full of shit. She was beginning to see she wasn't any of the things he claimed. It wouldn't be gone overnight. It hadn't been driven into her head overnight. She was gaining on it, though, and much better than she was months ago. With practice and patience with herself, she'd have the damage that she let him do to her self-esteem in no time. It was time to start living.

To help her drown out the voice of doubt, Marlina focused on Gabriel. The sight of the muscles bunching and flexing under his tight t-shirt was magnificent. His trim waist tapered into a V, and she last night she felt those sexy cut muscles along his hips that led down to his magnificent cock. She's seen him nude once when she stayed the night with Mia, that last summer when he was a man, and he was big. Really big. Her body tightened in anticipation of feeling all those hard, thick inches deep inside her.

Her gaze dropped down to his tight, bitable ass. She'd always appreciated a man with a nice ass. *Male perfection.* Everything about him was perfect. It was crazy. Seriously, a man really shouldn't be allowed to walk around looking as good as him.

When they passed the main house, she frowned. "Gabriel—I thought we were going to your house."

"We are," he said, squeezing her hand gently.

She was confused. "But didn't we just pass it?"

"I don't live in the main house anymore."

"Oh." The fact that he didn't live in the main house was awesome, and it made her feel a million times better about screwing him in the middle of the afternoon.

Glancing over his shoulder at her, he said, "My house is just far enough away from the main house." Grinning, his eyes turned hot again. "*Non preoccuparti*. No one will hear us," he said with a wink. The combination of his words and that devilish grin had her heart tripping over itself.

"I wasn't thinking that," she denied, her face flaming.

Looking up, Marlina could see he was making a beeline for the beautiful two-story villa made from stone. The windows were all modern, weatherproofed, and the startling white frames looked so beautiful against all the different stones used to make up the house.

Pulling open the front door, Gabriel ushered her through it. She gasped, stopping just inside. The floor beneath her feet was red brick, something she hadn't expected from such a modern looking house. Usually, if the floors weren't wood, they were tile. Above her head, the thick 2x4 beams, which held the ceiling up, matched the color of the brick flooring. To her left, there sat a large black sofa and a matching loveseat situated on a large, multi-colored rug. The coffee table and end tables that framed the furniture were mahogany, setting off the red brick and red beams across the ceiling. To her right, there was a smaller, more formal sitting room, which she assumed he used for business, like most people who owned a house this large.

"Wow, Gabriel," she said in awe.

Walking over to the large window, she looked out over the immaculate vineyard that had been in his family for generations, sweeping over the Tuscan countryside. "This place is beautiful. I used to explore all along your property with Mia, but I don't remember this place," she stated.

"You wouldn't remember it, not like this anyway." He grabbed her hand and pulled her behind him as he climbed the stairs. At the top of the stairs, he turned left and walked down the second story hallway until they reached the third door, which was a set of beautiful, frosted glass double doors. Pushing them open, he explained, "I had it restored a few years ago. You'd remember it being a ruin, with a—"

"Heavy wooden door, no roof, the left wall missing, and the courtyard in ruins," she finished his sentence. She was shocked that this was the same place. Crossing the room and stepping closer to the railing, she looked down into the courtyard. "You did this?"

He nodded, a little smirk of pride on his face. "*Sì*. I also remodeled the caretaker cottage closer to the vineyard. I live here and sometimes use that one as a guesthouse." He smiled. "Mia likes to stay there when she comes to visit. Gives her and her husband privacy."

"Privacy is important," she chuckles. "There's no way anyone would guess this beautiful home was once a pile of ruins. It's an amazing restoration." Taking a deep breath, she looked around again. "I'd like to see the caretaker cottage too. Mia and I used to play there."

He closed the shutters, plunging them into darkness. Pulling her back into the room with him, he continued. "I found the photos of what it looked like originally, and the man I called specialized restoration. He keeps it authentic but mixed with modern design too."

Still awestruck by the revelation of what this beautiful home used to look like, she hadn't been paying attention until the bedroom door shut, and a rustle of movement sounded from behind her. Her breath hitched. She wanted to turn around to see what Gabriel was doing, but she was chicken.

The scrapping of a match across the side of a matchbox sounded a moment before the flare of a brief golden light illuminated the darkness. Gathering her nerve, she turned around, her gaze falling on Gabriel as he lit candles across the fireplace mantle.

"Candles?" she asked in surprise.

"I find candles create a softer, gentler environment." Walking back over to the door, he locked it before turning back around to face her. Slipping his hands into the pockets of his jeans, he leaned back against the door, gaze fastened on her. "Relaxing and soothing," he growled in a low voice. "And erotic," he added with a devious glint in his eyes.

Taking a moment to calm herself, she looked around the room. The shutters to the balcony effectively blocked out all the light from outside. She could just imagine the doors open, the night outside alive with the sound of crickets and a cool summer breeze blowing through the room, billowing the sheer white curtains.

As she continued to gaze around the room, her eyes fell upon the large king-sized bed, with a black comforter. She pictured being curled up next to Gabriel come morning, her back to his chest and his arm around her waist. Their legs would be tangled together with the thin white sheet draped over their hips. They'd be exhausted and sleeping in after a long night of making love several times.

Releasing a deep breath, she took in the rest of the room. Resting against the wall across from the foot of the bed was a beautiful armoire. On the wall, on either side of the armoire, hung two gorgeous landscape paintings of grapevines. Reds, greens, and purples made up row after row of vines stretching toward the horizon in each picture. However, in the second painting, the focal point seemed to be much different. In the first painting, the vines offset the stone ruins of what used to be a cottage, while the second painting showcased the main house of a vineyard—this house, to be exact.

One was painted to show the beautiful colors of the sunrise, and the other was painted to show the colors of the sunset.

I know these paintings, she thought to herself.

Turning to face Gabriel, mouth agape, she asked, "Where'd you get these?"

With his intense gaze focused on her again, it made her feel just as antsy as before. "Your Nonna gave them to me."

"What?" Studying the paintings, a moment longer, she turned back to him. "I painted those—"

"The last summer you were here," he stated matter of fact. Giving her a single nod, he folded his arms over his chest. "I asked her for them, and she agreed."

She was beginning to hate it when he took that pose. His thick biceps pressing against the short sleeves of his thin t-shirt made her mouth water. They were an intelligence killer. Clearing her throat, she tore her gaze away from his arms and focused on his eyes. "And she just gave them to you?"

"Why wouldn't she?" he asked, pushing himself away from the door. He crossed over to her with slow, calculated steps. "I wanted them," he stated. By this point, he was standing so close she could feel the heat from his body seeping into her.

Shivering at his nearness, her gaze shifted to the paintings. They were done when she was just 15-years-old, during the last summer she had spent here. There was such boldness and passion in each brushstroke. Looking back, she remembered wanting to see and paint everything. It was almost like she knew it would be her last summer here.

She tried to capture everything, every single detail about the beautiful place she'd come to love and think of as her real home. There were so many things she wanted to remember about being here. She figured painting it would always keep it in her mind, and she would remember the beauty and simplicity of a place where she was so happy. Regrettably, Vivian wouldn't allow her to take the paintings back to the States with her because this part of her life was over. Deep down, Marlina believed her mother knew she would lose her to the simple life here. The history behind the two paintings only meant something to her, no one else. Or at least that's what she thought.

Adam, like her mother, always believed her paintings were a waste of time. So, she was shocked to find them in Gabriel's home. "I can't believe she gave them to you," Marlina uttered.

Lightly trailing his fingertips down her arm, he circled her wrist gently. "That's not entirely true. She offered to give them to me, but I refused. I bought them."

She sucked in a quick breath. "My grandmother sent me money four years after I left here." It was a lot of money, and most of it paid her way through college. She turned to face him, awestruck by the revelation. "That was from you?"

Keeping his fingers around her wrist, he turned her hand over and brought her hand up to his mouth. "Yes," he whispered, his dark gray eyes remaining locked on hers as he brushed his lips over the delicate skin.

Trapped in his gaze, she sank her teeth into her bottom lip and bit back a moan. "Why?"

"Why what?" he whispered, gently scraping his teeth across her flesh.

She moaned, unable to contain it any longer. "Why did you want them?"

A small smile pulled at his lips as he reached out, brushing his thumb across her cheek. Carefully, he tucked a strand of hair behind her ear. "*Perché li hai fatto tu.*" Gabriel ran his hands up both of her arms, rough calluses scraping across soft skin, causing the most erotic sensations to dance through her. Cupping her neck, he pressed his thumbs under her jaw and gently pressed her head back. "Because you made them." Lowering his head, he feathered his lips along her jaw and up toward her ear. "Having them, was like having a piece of you here with me." Wrapping his arm around her, he rested his hand at the small of her back and pulled her body tightly against him. "Do you know how many times I've laid in my bed, staring at those pictures, thinking about you?"

Her eyelids fluttered. "How many?" she asked, closing her eyes.

Kissing his way across her jaw and up to her lips, he placed a light kiss to her lips. "Every night," he rasped. A long pause stretched between them before he finally spoke. "Do you want to change your mind about this? About us?"

Pressing herself more fully against him, she rested her hands on his chest, and the feel of his body pressed against hers was intoxicating. He was so hard, everywhere. From his chest to the hard length of his cock, pressing against the junction between her thighs, there was no denying his need for her. She wanted this to happen for so long, and now that it finally was, she could barely believe it. Gabriel was actually touching her, kissing her, and he was about to make love to her, which was something she'd been dreaming about since the summer she turned fifteen.

"I don't want to change my mind," she sighed breathlessly. The hungry look in his eyes made her so hot, she felt like she was going to burst into flames any second. "I want you."

"Good," he growled, capturing her mouth in a hard, demanding kiss.

TUSCAN HEAT

Chapter 9

Marlina mewled, wrapping her arms around Gabriel's neck. It wasn't a gentle kiss. It was rough, demanding, and so, so good. This kiss was all lips, tongue, and teeth as they tried to taste every crevice of each other. It had been so long since that summer when she was fifteen, and they stole that kiss in the vineyard—that kiss, her first kiss.

Gabriel's fingers tightened in her hair, using the leverage to pull her head back, so he could take complete possession of her mouth. His tongue tangled with hers, caressing, swirling. His hand slid down her hip and over her ass, reaching around and squeezing one firm globe roughly. Dragging her hips up against his, so close together, his hard cock pressed into her abdomen, made her all hot and needy. Gabriel changed the angle of the kiss, taking it deeper, more aggressive as he ground his hips against hers. Her nipples scratched back and forth against the thin material of her dress; the erogenous zone sent pleasure shooting through her like a rocket, making her knees go weak and turned her legs to jelly.

"Gabriel," she whimpered, breaking the kiss. Reaching down, she grasped the bottom of his shirt and pushed it up his chest. He pulled back only long enough to reach behind his head, grasp the material of his shirt and yank it off. Tossing it forgotten behind him, he swooped down and just as quickly had her back in his arms, his demanding kiss once again sweeping away all rational thought.

His tongue dipped in and out of her mouth in an erotic dance that mimicked what he would be doing to her body very soon. Her head spun. Every inch of her body tingled from heightened sensitivity. God, the man could kiss. Running her hands up his side, her palms skated over his defined obliques, across his chest, and down his incredibly chiseled six-pack. His skin was so smooth and so hot. *Delicious.* Marlina couldn't wait to run her tongue over every part of his body, couldn't wait to feel every naked inch of his skin pressed up against hers. The thought alone sparked a heat inside her, so intense, scorching her from the inside out.

"Wow," she muttered, greedily taking in the sight of his bare torso. Intricately detailed tattoos twisted up both arms wrapping around his shoulders and dancing up his neck in beautiful designs that she couldn't quite make out. Those strong hands clenched at his sides, making the letters across his knuckles stand out even more. The man was incredibly built, and with the tattoos stretching over his tanned torso, yeah, her mouth was fucking watering. Seriously, the man looked like he'd been airbrushed. His golden skin glistened in the candlelight, muscles bulging, strong legs. He was like a Greek god come to life. *Dangerous, charming, perfect.*

Those broad shoulders of his had always turned her on, and those muscular biceps and forearms had thick veins that stood out clearly underneath the skin, delicious and yet another hot button for her. And that abdomen, god, he didn't have a six-pack, he had an eight pack; the dips shadowed in the low-light. His obliques flexed with each breath, while the deep, defined V running over his hips and down into his jeans had her anxious to run her tongue along the indentation.

"Are you just going to keep staring at me?" he growled. "Or are you going to make things even?" He motioned to her dress.

She smiled, slowly tugging her skirt up her thighs, teasing him with every inch she revealed. "Do you really think that's fair? I mean," she unclasped the first button on her dress, followed by the second. "I take this off, and I'm left standing in only a black lacy thong."

He swallowed hard. "Thong?" he asked in a gravelly voice.

One hand held the bottom of her dress at her hip and the other continued unbuttoning her sundress with the other. "Mm-hm." Shrugging her shoulders slightly, her dress fell to her elbows, exposing her bare breasts.

Gabriel sucked in a sharp breath. "Seems I have more clothes on now," he rasped, stepping closer to her. "How do you think we should fix that?"

Reaching out, she grasped his beltloop and pulled him even closer to her. "Taking these off would be a good start," she whispered as, she popped open the button on his jeans.

"I think so too." Reaching out, he cupped her breasts, skimming his thumbs across her hard nipples.

She held her breath in anticipation as he bent his head, capturing the hard peak in his warm mouth. A soft mewl escaped her as she buried her fingers in his hair, holding him firmly to her breast. His mouth was hot and wet, and felt incredible. God, Gabriel had her body on fire and her thong soaked. If she were to rub her thighs together in just the right way, her swollen clit would brush against the cloth of her panties, and she'd probably come; that's how turned on he had her.

Swinging her hips, she shrugged the dress off until it pooled in a soft pile at her feet. Gabriel ran his rough hands down her sides, over her hips. Kneeling, he hooked his fingers in the sides of her thong. "These need to come off," he growled, looking up at her.

She simply nodded her agreement.

He smiled, slowly dragging her soaked thong down her curvy legs, each new inch revealing more of her deliciousness to his gaze. "*Si bellissima,*" he groaned, pressing a smoldering kiss to the bare skin just above her pussy.

"Gabriel," she whimpered, goosebumps breaking out across her skin as he trailed his lips ever so slowly over her hipbones ever so slowly, across her lower abdomen, and down her thighs, first one then the other. Holding onto his shoulders for balance, she carefully stepped out of her panties. Once free, he tossed them aside with the rest of their clothing, fully intent on pocketing them later.

"That's right, baby," he rasped, running his hands up her legs, starting at her ankles. "Say my name." Slipping his fingers between her legs, he slowly ran his fingers through her slick heat, caressing her clit with the tips of his fingers. Crying out, Marlina dug her fingernails into his shoulders. Pleasure unlike anything she'd ever known, zinged through her, stoking the flames burning inside her hotter.

The excitement, the ecstasy, the passion of being with Gabriel—was so new. It made all of her other sexual experiences seem so technical and passionless. What she was experiencing with Gabriel was different. It was hot, wild, overwhelming, and so fucking intense.

Surging to his feet, Gabriel wrapped his arms around her waist, capturing her mouth. Pushing his tongue past her lips, he didn't just kiss her; he devoured her and demanded her response. Her head spun. Every muscle trembling and her limbs weakening, refusing to hold up her weight. Grasping his hair, she yanked his head back, smiling at the sound of pleasure that rumbled from him. Nipping along his strong jaw, Marlina flicked his lobe with the tip of her tongue before sucking it into her mouth and letting it slip back out through her teeth. Kissing down his neck, she dragged her teeth over his tendon at the base of his throat before seductively running her tongue along his collarbone and shoulder.

"You're driving me crazy," he growled, lying her down on the soft bed. Wedging his knee between her thighs, he gently nudged them apart before settling his weight on top of her. Kissing her neck, he nipped the sensitive skin below her ear before soothing the wounded skin with his tongue. "*Voglio assaggiare ogni centimetro di te*," he whispered in her ear. "I've been waiting for this moment for twenty years." Kissing his way down her neck and chest, over her breasts to her nipples, he firmly captured the hard peak between his teeth. Sucking hard as he flicked the sensitive tip with his tongue.

Grasping the black comforter beneath them, Marlina gasped, arching her back into him. "W—what did you say first?" she panted.

Switching to her other breast, Gabriel showed it the same attention with tongue and teeth that he had shown the other. By the time Gabriel released her breast from his wicked mouth, Marlina was writhing and panting beneath him. Kissing a path over to her sternum and down her flat belly, he whispered, "It means, I want to taste every inch of you."

His calloused fingertips caressed the smooth skin of her upper thighs; he softly dipped his tongue into her belly button before kissing his way down her abdomen. Moving downward, he shouldered her legs apart before lying on his stomach between her soft, supple legs.

Rising on her elbows, she focused solely on the sexy man between her thighs. The sight of his dark head between her legs amped her arousal up about a thousand degrees. Her breathing kicked up a notch as heat flushed her chest and cheeks. It was a little embarrassing to admit, but this right here, was new to her.

The mere thought of her past had her attempting to close her legs. Gabriel's broad shoulders prevented her. Staring at her bare pussy, he licked his lips like a starving man. Marlina's core clenched with need at the hungry look on his face. As he dropped his head between her thighs, she held her breath in anticipation.

With the first flick of his tongue, Marlina moaned loudly, her head falling back on her shoulders. *Oh god, that feels fucking amazing.* Fingers brushing past her delicate folds, they slid up her slit until his thumb grazed her throbbing clit. Molten pleasure shot through her, and she gasped, legs trembling.

Completely focused on what he was doing, Gabriel expertly rubbed the small nub in a circular motion. Her vision tunneled, seeing only him. Lifting his gaze to watch her, he applied more pressure to her clit until she whimpered in need.

"Do you like that?" he asked, his voice husky and low.

Marlina nodded, unable to speak due to the ecstasy blasting throughout her body. A storm was gathering, swirling in her center, one that Gabriel was creating and feeding with each new stroke. Without warning, Gabriel inserted one long finger inside her wet pussy.

"Oh god," she cried out, pushing herself into his hand. She wanted more; needed more. "Gabriel, please," she pleaded.

Another long stroke, followed by his tongue flicking and circling her clit, sent her body into uncontrollable spasms. Whimpering, she fell back onto the bed. Fighting to catch her breath, it wasn't long before he was fucking her with his tongue, sucking her clit in-between thrusts. She was writhing on the bed; head thrust back, comforter gripped tightly in her fists as ecstasy skating across her nerves, making every cell in her body come to life.

Gripping her ass, he lifted her closer to his mouth. Redoubling his efforts, he licked and sucked, teased, and flicked. "Gabe…oh god…yes…right there," she panted. "Oh, god, I'm gonna come," the last word left her mouth on a high-pitched squeal of pleasure. Gasping, she lifted her hips, her thighs quaking. Meanwhile, Gabriel's strong fingers dug into the soft flesh of her ass, unwilling to allow her to escape until he was completely satisfied.

Squeezing her eyes closed, her hips tilted up against his hand of their own accord. Toes pressing into the bed, the tension built inside her until it reached a breaking point. *Just a little more,* she silently prayed. *I'm almost there…just a little more.* Sucking her clit into his mouth once again, his teeth gently skimmed over the sensitive flesh as he simultaneously thrust two fingers deep inside her.

Eyes closed, she opened her mouth to scream, but only a small whimper escaped. Arching her back, her muscles locked as the pleasure consumed her. Her body trembled, thighs clasped tightly against Gabriel's head, which was still buried between her legs as he licked every drop of pleasure from her.

Panting like she'd just run a marathon, she fell back on the bed, her legs falling open in exhaustion. "Wow," she laughed breathlessly. "That was amazing."

"*Sei così bella quando vieni,*" he said as he kissed his way up her body, gently nipping at her lips.

Grinning like a fool, she softly ran her hands over his shoulders and down his back as he settled his weight on top of her. "What does that mean?"

Resting his weight on his elbows, he stared down into her eyes. His eyes twinkled in the golden candlelight. "You know, I'm going to have to teach you Italian. It isn't sexy if I have to translate." His strong abdomen muscles flexed as he let out a deep laugh.

Marlina opened her mouth to say something smart assed back, but he swooped down and captured her lips before any words could be spoken. A squeak of surprise sounded, giving him the perfect opportunity to slip inside, tongue swirling erotically with hers. His hard cock pressed against her thigh, twitching with eagerness. Tilting her head back, she sucked on his tongue. Spreading her legs wider, she silently begged him to come inside.

"Marlina," he whispered against her lips. "Wait."

"I don't want to wait," she said, raising her hips in protest. "I'm on birth control, and I haven't been with anyone but Adam," she moaned again. "Fuck me, please."

Groaning, he lowered his head, resting his forehead against her shoulder. "I haven't been with anyone for a while, and I've always used protection." He raised his head, gazing at her. "I don't want anything between us," he whispered.

She nodded, grinding her hips up against his. "Me either. Please," she begged. "Now."

With one hand clasped on her hip, the other grasped her thigh, gently lifting her leg over his hip. The hot, swollen head of his hard cock pressed against her entrance. Angling his hips, he pressed forward, sinking just the tip inside before slowly pulling back out. "Fuck, you're tight," he groaned, pressing his lips against her temple.

Whimpering in frustration, Marlina tilted her hips, trying desperately to take him deeper inside her. She'd never been desperate to feel a man inside of her, not to the point that she would beg for it. She'd do a lot more than beg for Gabriel to sink himself deep. Then again, she'd never experienced an all-consuming need like this. "Please," she begged.

Kissing her hard, he sank into her in one fast, unyielding thrust. Breaking the kiss, she cried out, her hands grasping his back, nails digging into his skin. Remaining still for a moment, he buried his face against her throat.

Shifting her hips, she winced. He was bigger and thicker than she expected. The burn from her body stretching to accommodate his girth was uncomfortable, but in a pleasurable way. Experimentally, she rotated her hips.

Gabriel's body tensed at the sensation. "Marlina," he said in a hoarse voice, his hands grabbing her hips to halt her movement. "Wait."

She didn't want to wait. The burn was already fading, and the need to move was consuming her. Something had to quench this hunger he'd fanned to life inside her. Wrapping her other leg around him, she rotated her hips again. Pleasure shot through her.

"Oh, yes," she breathed, repeating the motion again and again. "You feel so good."

Digging his fingers into her hips, he groaned harshly. Moving his hips back slowly, he thrust forward in one hard stroke. Moaning, she lifted her legs higher up his sides, tilting her pelvis to take him deeper. With Gabriel's next thrust, the pleasure felt incredible. He was so deep inside her, deeper than she thought possible, his cock sliding across that sensitive piece of flesh of hers. Eyes rolling back in her head, she nearly screamed when he repeated the action. The pleasure was so intense all she could do was whimper and hold on tight.

Picking up his speed, Gabriel thrust in and out of her in hard, fast movements. Gasping, she softly ran her hands down his back and cupped his ass with both hands. His firm ass flexed with every thrust. Unable to control herself, her hips rose, meeting him thrust for thrust as the sound of skin slapping against skin mixed with each of their moans.

"*Cazzo*," he groaned against her neck, sucking on the tender skin just below her ear. "You feel so good."

Closing her eyes tightly, her head rolled from side to side as she clutched him tightly to her. She was right on the edge. All she needed was a little push. "Faster," she gasped. "Harder."

A growl rumbled from deep within Gabriel's chest as he picked up speed. His abs flexed against her with every stroke as he pumped into her picking up the pace, just like she wanted. Digging her heels into his ass, her hands grasped onto his shoulders and held on tightly as she moved up the bed with the force of his hips slamming against her. Gasping, her eyes rolled back behind her closed lids, toes curling as her orgasm hit her hard. Head arching back against the pillow, she cried out in erotic bliss.

He slid into her over and over, riding her throughout the tidal wave of pleasure. Every muscle in her body was tense, thighs shaking, the pleasure so good it was almost painful. Pushing into her again, stretching her, it felt so good. Groaning, Gabriel froze, his body going rigid. Cock pulsing inside her, the first jet of warmth shot deep inside her. She felt sheer enjoyment at the sound of Gabriel groaning in pleasure, while shooting his come deep inside of her.

Grinding his hips against her, Gabriel drew out every single ounce of pleasure. Breathing heavily, and completely sated, he collapsed onto the bed next to her. Not a sound could be heard, except for their breathing.

Listening to Gabriel breathe, Marlina couldn't help but notice how much it sounded as though he'd just run a marathon. Of course, after that rendezvous in the sheets, she probably did too. Turning her head slightly to look at Gabriel, Marlina was surprised to see his stormy gray eyes were focused on her. To say she didn't quite know how to react would be an understatement. The only man she'd ever been with was Adam, and their first time was in college. Fumbling in the dark in her cramped dorm room with her roommate asleep just across the room, they were forced to be quiet. In the darkness of her dorm room, she couldn't exactly make out Adam's face, and he'd left right after, so there was no awkward 'after sex' talk. Not like now.

It was odd—that simple, primitive act of him coming inside her made her feel more connected to him than she ever had with Adam. How that was possible, she didn't know. But all the bad experiences with Adam slammed back into her memory. The act of sex as a duty as a married couple, no intimate touching, and his refusal to eat her out because it was vulgar and disgusting, came rushing back.

Nerves swirled in her stomach. The warmth of anxiety spread from her gut and up to her chest as her heartbeat faster. As the heat continued to spread up to her face and across her cheeks, the pounding of her heart became deafening her ears. Her breaths grew choppier. However, this time it had nothing to do with pleasure, but fear.

As her breaths sawed in and out of her lungs, she struggled to calm her nerves. *What am I supposed to do? Will things be different between us now that we've had sex? Was this a mistake? Should I get up and leave?* The questions flooded her mind, waging an internal war that had her tense and on edge.

Women have sex all the time. Gabriel has sex all the time, she told herself in an effort to calm her nerves. Bad move because that stupid thought opened the door for all kinds of scenarios to play through her self-conscious mind. *This isn't good.* She was really panicking, and now she could add fucking jealousy to the list of irrational thoughts invading her subconscious. *Why am I even jealous? We aren't together.* Gabriel made no promises to her. Marlina wasn't one to get wrapped up in a man who didn't want a commitment. Or was she? *Fuck, I should've had more sex, then I might know what to do.*

Breaking eye contact, she turned her head to focus on something else—anything else. Staring at the mantle above the fireplace, she tried to gather her thoughts in an attempt to make sense of what had happened and what she was feeling. It wasn't like she regretted sleeping with Gabriel. It was beautiful, amazing—mind-blowing even. Marlina never knew sex could be like that. It certainly hadn't been anywhere near as good with her ex-husband. Unlike Adam, everything with Gabriel was perfect.

That being said, there was just one question that needed to answer, *Why the hell am I freaking out?*

TUSCAN HEAT

Chapter 10

Gabriel felt the best he'd ever felt in a long damn time. He was naked in bed with the woman he'd been fantasying about since he was, well, a kid. He'd say teenager, but his fascination with Marlina began when they were just children. The beautiful little girl with the sad eyes captured his attention, and being his sister's best friend; it gave him plenty of time to chase after her. No matter what he did, she never seemed to notice him.

Women of all ages were falling all over him since he shot up and filled out when he was sixteen. After that, if he wanted a woman all he had to do was flirt with her, sometimes not even that, and she'd pretty much fall all over him. He wasn't arrogant; it was the truth.

He always flirted with Marlina, but she'd always roll her eyes, snort, and walk away. He still tried, but it never got him anywhere. The summer he turned eighteen, everything changed. In the beginning of that summer, she came over for a family dinner. She was dressed in a beautiful pale-yellow dress with sunflowers all over it. He remembered every detail of her makeup, how her hair blew in the breeze, and every curve of her supple body in that dress.

Smiling, he flirted with her, expecting her to roll her eyes like she always did. But it didn't happen. Instead, she smiled and teased back. He'd been so stunned that he didn't react right away; he just stood there like an idiot. Another coy smile from her and a caress down his arm from her soft, delicate hand put him back on his game. Except it wasn't a game, not with her.

They flirted back and forth all that summer. Everything changed between them at his eighteenth birthday party. While they were making out, he felt like he was going to explode. He was so fucking happy. He could barely believe he finally had his hands on her. After she left that summer and never came back, he was heartbroken. He was confident they would see each other again, tried to track down her phone number, but it had changed. He wrote her letter after letter only to have them returned in bulk months later. He waited, counting down the days until she turned eighteen, certain that she would find a way to contact him, but she didn't.

When he heard she was getting married, his world stopped. Even though it had been years since he'd seen her, a strange emptiness seemed to take precedence in his heart. Gabriel tried to fill the void, tried to move on with an endless parade of women, hoping he'd find one to fill the hole. Then the day came when he accepted that the emptiness may never go away. He was convinced that the love of his life, his soul mate was the girl he knew and the woman he lost. Over the years, he learned to enjoy being with other women without comparing them to Marlina. After a time, he managed to convince himself that what he felt for her was nothing more than a childhood crush. Then she walked back into his life.

The second he laid eyes on her, the old feelings that he'd convinced himself were in his imagination came rushing back like a tsunami. It was like no time had passed at all. Being with her again, in that same kitchen, they'd spent so much time in as children; he knew the truth. *Lei era il suo destino*, she was his destiny—the other half of him, his soul mate.

Turning his head as they lay naked in bed together, he looked at her. Her olive-colored skin glistened in the flickering candlelight. Strands of highlighted caramel colored hair stuck to her sweat-dampened forehead and across her cheeks. He watched as her chest rose and fell just as rapidly as his as they struggled to catch her breath.

Dio, she is so damn beautiful, he thought to himself. The mere sight of her had his cock coming to life for round two.

Panic flashed in her eyes as she sank her white teeth into her bottom lip. He frowned just as she turned her head away from him. His body tensed as the heat of anger flashed through him. Her panic was a blow to the gut. He knew exactly what was happening, and it pissed him off.

Slipping off the bed, he walked around to the other side without bothering to cover himself. Stopping right in front of her, he said, "*Che cazzo sta succedendo? Cos'è questa merda di spalla fredda?* Since you don't understand very much Italian, I'll translate for you." Taking a deep breath, he clenched his hands into fists and tried to calm himself. "What the fuck is going on? What is with this cold shoulder shit? You look like a deer in headlights, for Christ sake." He wanted, no, he needed to know what the fuck was going on in her head.

Her gaze remained locked on his feet as she sat up, wrapping the sheet around her body. "I don't know what you're talking about," she said, feigning innocence.

Reaching down, he grasped her chin firmly and jerked her head up to meet his gaze. His lips flattened into a thin line as his breathing kicked back up.

"Bullshit!" he snapped, unable to stop himself. "Don't lie to me, not after fucking like we just did," he scolded.

She winced, jerking her chin from his grip as her green eyes burned with anger.

Good. At least I knew there is some emotion behind that cold façade she is trying to throw up.

"Do you have to be so crude?" she snapped right back before standing.

"What would you call it?"

Bending down, she grabbed her dress off the floor. "Nothing."

Nothing? Fuck that! There is no way she is just going to fuck me and then leave, acting like what happened between us was nothing. It was everything. He'd given up hope of ever seeing her again, of having her like this, and there was no fucking way he was going to let her walk out of here because of the shit her ex did. That had nothing to do with him. Nothing to do with them. After kissing her lips, touching her skin, and finally having her body, there was no way in hell he was going to let her walk away from him. Not without a fight. Gabriel was used to getting what he wanted, and there was nothing he wanted more than Marlina.

Deep down, he knew there was only one way to make this woman listen to what he had to say. Yanking her dress from her, he held it over his head. She played right into his hand and jumped for it. Jerking his sheet from her body, he quickly bent down to grab her underwear. Rolling them into a ball, he walked over to his balcony and opened the shutters before stepping outside.

"Gabriel, give me back my clothes," she demanded.

Stopping at the railing, he turned sideways to look at her and smirked. "No." With that, he dropped the bundle over the side. If she wanted to leave, she was going to have to do it naked.

A squeak of shock escaped her as she watched her clothing fall to the ground. "You can't just deny giving me my clothes." Her hands went to her hips, unintentionally thrusting out those luscious breasts he'd worshiped with his hands, mouth, and teeth. *Fuck, she is captivating. Especially standing there all pissed off like she could kick my ass. I'd even let her, as long as that naked body of hers was rubbing up against me, tits bouncing. Just to rile her up more, I'd even grab a handful of ass.* The mere sight of her standing before him naked and angry had his mind wandering. Yeah, he could get into her being angry at him, but not for something her bastard ex did.

"I'm not denying you your clothes," he said, motioning to the balcony. "If you want them, go and get them."

She narrowed her eyes. "I can't go out there naked, and you know it. Your entire family will see me."

"Then I guess you will just have to stay up here and talk to me." His voice was hard, and he knew his gaze was too, but he didn't care. He wanted answers.

Stiffening, her gaze fell from his as she grabbed a pillow from the bed and pressed it against her body. "I know what this is," she raised her gaze to his, her steely determination evident. "I know how this works, and I wasn't going to make a big deal about it. But you didn't have to throw my clothes out the window," she snapped.

"What do you know?" he barked, reaching for her.

Evading him, she backed up, her naked ass hitting the wall. "That you just want me to leave."

Slamming his hands against the wall on either side of her head, he pressed in close to her. "Let me ask you one thing, why in the fuck would I throw your clothes outside if I wanted you to leave?" He hoped his harsh tone would get his point across. Anger was flowing through him. He clenched his jaw so hard his teeth ached.

She was trapped. Brilliant green eyes wide and locked on him, she stammered, "I-I—"

His cock stirred, the alpha male in him becoming excited over being dominant and in command of his woman. *Hmm, my woman,* he thought in approval. *Yeah, that felt right because that's exactly what she is—his woman.* If she thought she was going to fuck him and then walk away like nothing happened, like some one-night stand, she better re-think that shit. She was his, and he had no intention of letting her go again. Ever.

He continued to stare at her hard. "I'm waiting."

"I'm confused," she whispered. "I thought I was giving you what you wanted, what all men want."

"And what is it that you think all men want after sex?" Even though he was pissed off, her confusion and hurt eased his anger.

"Don't be cruel, Gabriel," she muttered, lowering her gaze.

Slipping his finger under her chin, he gently raised her head. Keeping her eyes downcast, Gabriel softly whispered, "Look at me." *Nothing.* "Marlina, look at me," he said more firmly. Slowly, she raised her gaze to his. Her beautiful green eyes sparkled with tears. At that moment, he knew it was going to take some work to win the trust of his little *farfalle*-butterfly. "You can trust me," he said softly.

Almost immediately, the vulnerability fled from her eyes, replaced by the fire he loved so much. He nearly breathed a sigh of relief. In truth, he preferred her anger to the lost look she had before. She was much stronger than she gave herself credit for.

"Don't talk to me like I'm some scared little animal." She narrowed her eyes on him. "How can you possibly tell me that I can trust you, when I don't know you? I don't know anything about you."

Taking her hand in his, he pressed her palm over his heart. With his other hand, he cupped her cheek. "You know me," he whispered. "You've always known me."

Sighing heavily, she shook her head. "The last thing any man wants is a commitment of any kind. Every woman knows that." Removing her hand, she pressed it against the pillow she still clutched to her chest.

"It's not just men," he argued.

"Fair enough." Nodding in agreement, she bit her lip gently and shrugged. "I figured if I just left afterward, it would save us from this awkward conversation."

"The awkward part of me telling you that this is just a casual thing, and that I don't want any kind of commitment because I'm playing around?" He would never understand American women and their willingness to settle for less than what they wanted just because it was what the man wanted. Italian women would just move on to the next man that wanted them and would appreciate them, because they knew there were plenty of men out there. For a woman as beautiful as Marlina, she would have no problem finding a man who was more than willing to give her everything she could ever ask for. Lucky for him, he was that man.

She gave a small smile. "It's playing the field. And yes."

"Why do you assume I want to…'play the field'? Have I said that to you?"

Marlina opened her mouth; no doubt to say yes, but then quickly closed it. A few moments passed before she finally spoke. "No. I guess you haven't, but like I said—"

"Ah, yes." He ran the tip of his index finger lightly down her arm. "All men want to take it easy." She chuckled again, but he knew she got his meaning. "That's not what I want."

Her eyes widened as she stared at him. Her breathing kicked up. "It's not?" she asked in shock.

He shook his head. "No."

"W-what *do* you want?" she stammered.

Smiling, he bent his head and brushed his lips over hers. "What I've wanted since we were children."

"And that's?"

"What happened between us was amazing, and it was something that I never thought would be possible after I heard you got married. Now that it has happened, and everything is possible," he shook his head, "I'm not letting you go again."

"Again?" She stared at him, mouth agape, eyes bigger than before. "You can't be serious."

"I'm very serious." He cut off any further conversation with a hard press of his lips against hers. Forcing his tongue into her mouth in a sensual slide. Groaning loudly, he ripped the pillow away from her, wrapped his arms around her satin soft, supple body, and pulled her in close. Her soft, firm breasts pressed against his hard chest, setting his blood on fire. Who the fuck was he kidding? His entire body was on fire. His cock was rock hard and ready to sink into her tight pussy.

Breaking the kiss, he panted, gently dragging his lips across her jaw and down her neck. "Marlina, I need you."

Sinking those white teeth into her soft bottom lip, had him biting back a groan or need. Those big eyes of her locked with his before slipping away to flicker over his features as she studied him. The tension in her shoulders begins to loosen, her body softening as she leans towards him. Her hips bump against his, softly dragging against his hard cock.

A deep groan rips from him as his head falls back on his shoulders. Just that small touch, that one crush had his body tightening with hunger. "Marlina," he choked out. "I…can't wait."

Wrapping her arms around his neck, she held tight before jumping up and wrapping her legs around his waist. "Then don't wait," she whispered seductively.

His hard cockhead rested against her hot, wet entrance. Tilting her hips slightly, she tried to thrust down on him. Gabriel grasped her hips firmly in his hands, stopping her. He hissed as the tip of his cock slid in half an inch.

"Gabriel," she whimpered, rotating her hips in an attempt to get her to go deeper, but his firm grip held her in-place.

"*Voglio bambino*." Sweat beaded his forehead, and his hips jerked up in reflex of wanting to sink into her warm, welcoming body. She was shredding his fucking control to pieces. "I want to, baby, desperately, but we can't yet."

"Why?" she whined.

"Because," he said, allowing himself to slip in just a little farther. "We need to talk about this," he groaned.

"We will," she panted. "Later." She pressed kisses down his neck, nipping along the way before sucking the skin over his pounding pulse into her mouth. Her muscles clenched around his swollen head, squeezing him, enticing him to sink the rest of the way. His hips jerked involuntarily.

"Fuck," he hissed, thrusting shallowly, his legs trembled with the strength it took to hold back from plunging balls deep. "You feel so fucking good."

Rotating her hips, she tightened her thighs around his hips. "Gabriel," she begged. "Please."

"You're mine," he said through clenched teeth, slipping farther into her warmth. Groaning, he dug his fingertips into her rounded hips. "Do you hear me?" Pulling his hips back, he slammed deep. "Mine." He wanted her to know this thing between them was true. They were real. She was his, and he was hers.

"Yes," she groaned, sinking her teeth into his shoulder, hard. He growled low in his throat. "Fuck me before I lose my mind."

The thin thread of his control broke. Thrusting up, he simultaneously pulled her down and buried his rock-hard cock deep inside her core. Her head fell back on her shoulders, a cry of pleasure exploding from her. Grunting, he turned his head and nipped her neck. He intended to leave his mark on every part of her body. Soon her heart was going to belong to him the way his heart had always belonged to her.

Gabriel didn't go slow; he couldn't. They both wanted fire and passion. The furious pace taking them to the euphoria they desperately reached for. Pressing her back into the wall, he pounded into her, his balls slapping against her ass as she bounced up and down on his hard cock. "Fuck yeah. You're so tight and hot," he groaned. "Wet."

Whimpering, she leaned forward, capturing his mouth. Her tongue stroked his before thrusting deep, just like he was doing to her body. "It's all for you. God, you make me so wet," she gasped against his lips. "You feel so good."

She wasn't just wet; she was fucking soaked. Her juices dripped down his cock and balls. Shit, he wasn't going to last long at this pace. Not with her cream sliding down his dick. She cried out, her nails sinking into his shoulder. Arching her neck back, her body tensed. Pussy clenching down around his cock so tightly she was strangling him, holding her control.

Holding her tighter against him, he hammered his hips up into her. The sound of skin slapping skin filled the room, along with the sweet scent of sweat and sex. He was going to come, and he was going to come hard. He could feel it building deep in his balls as tingles raced up his spine.

"*Fuck!*" he roared, slamming his hand against the wall by her head. Three more deep, hard thrusts, and he was there. Coming so hard, he saw stars. His body tensed, every muscle going rigid as his dick twitched inside her. Cum shot from his cock with such an explosion of intense pleasure, his knees nearly buckled. He had to fight just to remain on his feet as stream after stream shot deep inside her.

It was the longest orgasm of his life. Ecstasy ripping through him, zapping every ounce of energy he had. Aftershocks throbbed through him, fading slowly as he carefully lowered Marlina to her feet.

Panting, he laid his damp forehead on her shoulder. "*Porca puttana*," he rasped, pressing gentle kisses to her skin. "Is it just me, or was that better than the first time?"

She nodded, caressing his chest as they both caught their breath. "It was definitely better, and more intense." She was quiet for a moment before speaking once again. "I wonder if it will always be like this. You know—different, better, more intense."

Pulling back, he grinned at her, nodding in the direction of the bed. "There's only one way to find out."

TUSCAN HEAT

Chapter 11

Marlina smiled as she walked up the stone walkway her grandfather had set into the ground all those years ago, when he and Nonna were first married. Gabriel's large, rough hand was wrapped around her smaller, softer one. The warm air kissed her overheated skin. After their argument, she stayed with him for two days, rarely getting out of bed.

Waking up this morning, deliciously sore brought a smile to her lips and a little heat to her cheeks as she remembered everything they'd done over the last couple of days. Gabriel was still sleeping, curled up around her, his strong arm wrapped around her waist. The warm sunlight spilled into the room, and across the bed. For the first time in her life, she knew what it was like to wake up exhilarated because of good sex.

Gabriel ravished her in so many different ways; it made her stomach heat and clench just thinking about it. Sex seemed like a bad description. It was like sex, the really sexy, filthy kind that you only read about or watched in movies. Honestly, they had to have tried every position ever thought up. In the two days, she had stayed at his house, he'd done things to her she'd never experienced or heard of. He had her coming so hard, so many times, it was a wonder she could use her voice. Not kidding——full-on screaming.

Squeezing her hand, she turned her head and smiled up at him, her breath catching in her chest. Whatever force brought them back together, she was totally grateful for it. She didn't want to come back home yet, but reality was waiting. Sadly, there would be no warm body next to her, no kisses on the back of her neck to wake her while strong hands roamed her body, when she woke up in the morning. She liked having him next to her. It felt awesome having a man in bed with her that actually wanted to be there. God knows Adam sure didn't, at the end, they didn't even sleep in the same bed. Gabriel liked being with her, and he showed it in every caress, every kiss, every grunt, and every groan whispered against her ear.

Sighing, she stepped ahead of him to turn the corner of the house, leading into the back yard. He stopped her, pulling her back against him. Trying to keep the smile on her face, she looked up at him.

"What's wrong?" he asked, studying her face, concern in his eyes.

Forcing a bright smile, she shook her head. "Nothing."

Cocking his head, he gave her a disapproving look. "Marlina," he said sternly.

Her smile slipped as she looked away from his probing gaze. "I had a lot of fun yesterday and today." *Damn, why is telling him the truth so hard? It shouldn't be this difficult to say to a man you love. No, wait, love. Too strong?* She argued with herself mentally. *Cared about. Yeah, that sounded right. It shouldn't be that hard to tell a man you cared about that you weren't ready for your time to end?* For the millionth time, she wished she was more like Lil and could just express her feelings without thinking about it.

Grinning, he brushed his thumb across her cheekbone. "I did too. A lot." Leaning down, he placed a chaste kiss upon her lips. "Now, tell me why you look so sad."

Lifting her gaze to his, she opened her mouth to speak, but the words got stuck in her throat. At a loss, she simply shrugged.

His eyes narrowed slightly as he pressed his delicious lips into a thin, displeased line she'd seen often over the last forty-eight hours. "Marlina, tell me what's wrong." Pulling back, he kept his commanding gaze locked with hers. "Tell me."

"I just…" knots twisted in her stomach. "I enjoyed being with you." She smiled. "It was a lot of fun. Waking up tomorrow, without your arms around me, is just a little bittersweet." It wasn't exactly what she was thinking but close enough. She was more wondering when she would see him again. She knew he said things were different between them, but she knew often men said one thing and did another, especially when sex was involved. It wasn't something she was comfortable coming right out and asking.

"Bittersweet." He rose a dark eyebrow. "Who says you're not going to be right back at my house, and in my bed."

His words made her feel better, more secure in the future that included them together. The talk they had in his bedroom did wonders to help her fragile confidence, but there was still that doubting voice whispering shit to her, but she was determined to ignore it.

Wrapping his arms around her, he kissed her forehead. "I wasn't planning on you staying here tonight."

Pulling back, she stared up at him, thoroughly confused. "You weren't? Then why did you bring me home?"

"I have a business meeting tonight. After I finish, I planned on coming back here and talking you into coming home with me." Tucking her hair behind her ear, he added, "But now you've ruined the surprise."

"No," she rushed out, shaking her head. "The surprise isn't ruined. What surprise? I don't know what you're talking about." Rising on her tiptoes, she outlined his lips with the tip of her tongue before gently dipping inside. She caressed his tongue with hers before running over his teeth and retreating.

Groaning in frustration, the fire of desire turned his gray eyes stormy. Reaching out for her, he said, "Come back here."

Dancing away from him, she wagged her finger at him. "Nope. I've got to go get ready for tonight—and for you," she said. Making a circle with her finger, she added, "And *you* need to go to your business meeting and come back here as soon as it's over."

"You know, I've been trying to set up this meeting for a long time. If we can strike a deal, it will be very good for DeLuca Wines."

"That's great," she stated brightly, and she meant it.

Chuckling, he nodded. "Yes, but if I'd had you a few days ago, I'd have canceled it."

If it were possible to melt, she would've done so right at his feet. He always knew the right thing to say to put her insecurities at ease.

Slipping his hands into the pockets of his dark wash jeans, he winked at her. "I'll see you later, *Amore mio.*" Giving her a gentle kiss, he walked back the way they'd come.

Did he just call me his love? She thought in shock.

Biting her lip, she watched his broad back disappear from view. It wasn't the first time he'd said it to her over the last two days, but it was the first time she believed he meant it. Somehow, Gabriel made her believe in what Nonna always told her. *'Not every man is out there to get what he can from a woman and then drop her like she was nothing to him.'*

Squealing with joy, she nearly skipped around the house to the veranda where Lil always hung out. She couldn't wait to tell her what had happened. They'd talked for a few minutes while she was gone, just so her sister knew where she was and wouldn't worry, but she hadn't been able to tell her any of the *'juicy details,'* as Lil called it.

When Marlina turned the corner, she found her sister sitting at the worn, scarred oak table, reading a paperback novel with a couple on the cover. The woman's arms were wrapped around the man's neck with her legs around his waist. His back was bare, and his thick arms bulged from the strength of holding the woman up.

Memories of her and Gabriel in the same position flew through her mind. Her mouth went dry, and sweat trickled down the back of her neck, rolling down her spine. She shivered. *I can't wait to be in that position again*, she thought to herself. *Maybe I'll be pressed against a different wall this time. Man, tonight can't come fast enough.*

Clearing her throat, she strutted up to the table and sat down. Lil didn't even raise her gaze from the book. *Damn, she must be at a sex part.* It was the only time she didn't pay attention to anything going on around her. Lilian had always said, '*If you can't get it, you can read about it.*' In reality, she was talking about both romance and sex. Marlina cleared her throat again, louder this time.

Lilian's gaze shot up, and her mouth broke into a wide smile. "Well, hello, stranger," she greeted, setting the book down.

"Hello, sister," she said, looking at her fingernails like she needed a manicure. "How are you today?" Since she dated and married a loser, she never had the fun of playing coy and pretending she'd hold back the intimate details.

Taking off her glasses and setting them beside her book, Lil got a devilish glint in her eye before scooting her chair closer. "Since you didn't come home for two days and could barely talk for longer than two minutes at a time, I'm assuming everything went well."

She nodded. "Unbelievable," Marlina said breathlessly.

"Okay, Lina, spill it."

Giggling, which was a shock because she so wasn't a giggler, she leaned forward. "It was amazing, Lil. Mind-blowing, toe-curling, seriously orgasmic. Even just thinking about it. I mean, I never knew sex could be like that."

Marlina watched as her sister made a pumping motion with her arm. "Yes. About time you got sexed-up, the right way."

Shaking her head, Marlina bit her lip. "I don't know what Adam was doing, but it sure as hell wasn't that."

"And?"

"And what?" she asked, frowning.

"What else? How did you do it, and where?"

Marlina wrinkled her nose. She could see her sister was practically salivating for some details. "No," she said, grabbing a napkin off the table and throwing it at her. "I'm not sharing any details with you. Nasty," she joked.

"Nasty?" Lilian made a face. "Last time you had a look like this on your face—wait, you've never had this look on your face. I should get to have a few juicy details."

Thinking about it, she gave a nod. "Okay, fine," she agreed. "We didn't leave a surface in his house untouched."

"Yeah," Lil gave an excited little squeal.

"That's all you're getting."

Her face fell, and she frowned. "You're no fun," she chuckled, throwing the cloth napkin back at Marlina's face.

For the next several minutes, Lil chattered on, but Marlina wasn't really paying attention. Nope, she was thinking about later, when Gabriel came to get her. She needed some lingerie, but sadly, she didn't have any. At least not anything hot and sexy, designed to drive a man crazy. *Some sexy ass lingerie,* she thought with a wicked smile.

"I want to go shopping," she said suddenly, cutting her sister off.

Lilian frowned. "Shopping? For what?"

She shrugged. "Just something. Mia's store has nice lingerie, right?"

Her sister grinned. "Ah, I see. I know just the place." Standing up from the table, Lil said, "Well, sis, let's get out there and find something that will make Gabriel swallow his tongue."

Marlina giggled. "Let's do it." Having a sister to share this experience with was so awesome, and something she'd been completely deprived of most of her young adult life. This was going to be so much fun. *So, is thinking of Gabriel's face when he sees me in lingerie.* Life was good.

TUSCAN HEAT

Chapter 12

"Come on, Lina, just one little, itsy, bitsy detail," Lil pressed. She couldn't be satisfied with the one detail Marlina gave her earlier. She wanted more. "It doesn't even have to be nasty," Lilian pleaded as they walked through the cobblestone streets. "It can be romantic. It doesn't have to be dirty like the books I read."

"Hey, I can barely remember the details without blushing. Can you imagine me trying to tell you about it?" Marlina laughed. "You know what you need? A hot Italian man. Then you won't need my dirty replays. You'll have your own."

Holding up her hands, she shook her head. "A man? No way! I need one of those like I need a hole in the head. The last man I went out with yanked a strand of hair from my head and slipped it into his coat pocket. What do you think he was going to do with it? A voodoo doll, that's what."

Marlina crossed her eyes at her sister. "Lil, that was when Becca was three—almost ten years ago. Think you might get over that any time soon? I mean, look at me…after what Adam did, a man was the last thing I was thinking about. Coming here, seeing Gabriel, taking a chance was the best thing I ever did. And because of it, I now like sex. No, I *love* sex," she admitted. Surprisingly, her cheeks didn't even turn red. "Don't you miss sex?"

"I did the whole sex thing, Lina. Lots of sex." Lilian said, shaking her head.

Her mouth fell open as she turned to her sister. "What? You never told me you were dating anyone."

"I wasn't. Dating wasn't something I did."

Now she was confused. "But you said you were having lots of sex."

Lilian nodded. "I was. Casual sex, Lina. When I had an itch, I scratched it." Lilian stopped in front of the restaurant they were going to dine at. It was the same place Gabriel had brought her a few days ago. Lilian hadn't been to it, preferring to stay home and cook for herself, but Marlina knew she was going to love it.

"That sounds terrible, you know," Marlina snorted, pulling the door open.

"Why? Men have casual sex all the time. In relationships, they cheat; who needs all that drama. Not me," she sighed heavily. "Hell, Mark never stopped dating when we were together. He was always panting after any hot young thing shook her ass at him," she shrugged. "There's a lot to be said for casual sex. It makes you feel amazing, most of the time. And you don't get hurt because it has nothing to do with your heart."

As bad as it sounded, her sister did make sense. "You said you *were* having casual sex, as in not anymore?"

Lilian shook her head. "No. It got old," she paused. "And lonely."

Marlina smiled. "So, are you saying you're ready to get into a relationship now?" She had the perfect man in mind for her sister too, and she'd already checked around; Lucien wasn't seeing anyone.

"I wouldn't go that far."

Together they walked inside, Marlina shook her head. "Wasn't it you who told me just the other day not to close myself off to possibilities because of one douchebag?"

"Well, that's because you couldn't see what was right in front of your face."

"What about what's in front of your face?" she asked, taking in the lighting and the romantic atmosphere once again. This was turning out to be her favorite place to come and have a meal.

"There's nothing right in front of my face," Lil muttered, looking at her sarcastically. "Except some grumpy, uptight man who's a pain in my ass." Marlina laughed. Rolling her eyes, Lilian said, "Enough about me, I'd rather talk about how Gabriel makes you feel."

"Lil," she warned.

"Come on, Lina. I'm not talking dirty details. I'm talking about how he makes you feel inside—your heart, your emotions. You know, all that girly crap."

"Feelings, huh? Yeah, I can do that." *As soon as I figure out what I'm feeling.* "Hey, when I was here with Gabriel, he took me out on the veranda; we should go out there. It's so beautiful. It has golden twinkle lights and everything. I think I even hear music."

"Sure, lead the way," Lil hummed. "You seeing him again tonight?" She asked as they made their way toward the veranda.

Marlina nodded, walking through the main dining room, near the bar area. "Yeah. After his meeting, he is going to—" her sentence faltered abruptly. Heart skipping a beat, a lump formed in her throat. Her breathing grew labored, and her heart raced like she'd just run a marathon. She felt dizzy, and everything became surreal.

Not even six feet away, at the small table closest to the bar, sat Gabriel.

He was dressed in a fancy black sweater and black slacks, instead of the suit, he'd laid out before he'd left with her to walk her home. Seeing him here was startling enough but seeing the woman sitting in front of him was shocking. He was supposed to be having a meeting.

Her gaze slipped over the woman. She had to be at least five-ten from the amount of leg she could see under the table. The woman wore a white dress shirt, black skirt, and heels so high she looked like she could break her neck in them. Not to mention the soles were red, which meant they were really expensive. The woman was beautiful. She had long blond hair, tanned skin, high cheekbones, full lips, and big blue eyes, framed with long eyelashes made for flirting. Leaning over the table, there was no doubt in Marlina's mind that her ample cleavage was exposed to Gabriel.

She couldn't make out what they were saying, but Gabriel said something, and the woman laughed, making her look even more stunning. The candle in the middle of the table cast a romantic golden glow across the couple. They looked perfect together. This was the kind of woman Gabriel should be with. Someone glamorous, a woman that looked like she'd walked off the cover of a magazine. Not someone frumpy and lost, like her. Her heart sank.

"Marlina? Marlina?" Lilian said, snapping her fingers in front of her face. "What's with you?"

She opened her mouth to say something, but she'd lost the ability to speak. All she could do was stare at Gabriel and the woman sitting with him. He fucked her, and then lied to her. He lied so he could keep his date with the knockout in front of him. Anger and hurt battled for dominance.

Why even bother saying all the shit he said? Spouting beautiful lies, and for what? She'd already fucked him. He should've let her walk out the door like she wanted. He was nothing but a fucking player, just like she suspected all along. Tears burned her eyes, threatening to fall. For a moment, she considered just leaving, walking away, and never seeing Gabriel DeLuca again. *Maybe that is for the best,* she thought. But before she could really consider that option, her anger got the better of her.

Looking in the direction Marlina was staring, Lilian whispered, "Oh shit. Lina, now don't go jumping to conclusions. You don't know what is going on over there," she said, trying to get her to think rationally.

Something dark, ugly, and angry moved through her. She was so damn angry, more upset than she'd ever been in her life, more furious than when Adam looked at her and told her he never loved her. This was like a big, hard ball of fire threatening to burn her up.

Lilian grabbed her arm in an attempt to halt what she was sure was going to be a terrible idea. "Lina, don't do this. You don't know what this is," she hissed.

Looking down at her sister's hand wrapped around her bicep, she gritted her teeth. "Let me go."

"No," Lilian said firmly.

Jerking out of her sister's grasp, Marlina marched over to where Gabriel was laughing and joking with the leggy blond. He was acting like he didn't have a care in the world. "Hey," she said, strutting up to the table. "How's the meeting going?"

Halting in his conversation, Gabriel looked up at her. A small smile began to stretch across his lips, but it quickly froze, morphing into a frown. "Marlina, baby, what are you doing here?" He moved to stand, but she didn't give him a chance.Grabbing the wineglass in front of him, she flung the liquid in his face before smashing the glass on the ground next to him. "I can't believe I trusted you," she seethed. "You asshole, bastard, dick. There aren't enough bad things to call you. I hope you two are very happy," she spat, choking on the last word. Turning, she rushed out of the restaurant, ignoring Gabriel calling her name from behind her.

The warm night air hit her face, and she could feel the wetness streaming down both cheeks, dripping off her chin. Fuck it all, she'd lost the battle not to cry, after all. No use holding back now. Not bothering to brush her tears away, she made her way down the street.

She just wanted to get home, curl up into a ball, and cry. Marlina couldn't believe she'd been so stupid, so naïve as to think a man cared for her again.

What is wrong with me? Why do I keep letting this happen?

"Marlina, wait!" a deep voice yelled from behind her.

She kept pushing her way down the street and through the crowds of people. Gabriel was the last person she wanted to talk to. Besides, she didn't have the patience for any bullshit excuse he would come up with. Hell, she didn't even want to look at him.

"Marlina, stop!" His voice was right behind her now, and before she could evade him, he grabbed her arm and turned her to face him.

Yanking her arm away from him, she snapped, "Don't touch me!" She glared at him with all the anger and hurt boiling inside her. "Why?"

"*Donna, sei pazzo, cazzo?*" he snapped. "Are you fucking crazy? Why would you walk in there and act like that?" His brow furrowed, and she could see the frustration and embarrassment on his face from the scene she'd made. *Good.*

"What is wrong with me?" she yelled back. "You have some nerve! You were supposed to be at a meeting tonight, Gabriel. Remember? You fucking lied to me!"

"I didn't lie to you," he growled, stepping closer to her. "That *was* the fucking meeting I was telling you about."

She laughed, full out laughed, making sure it sounded every bit as mocking as the stupid lie he was telling her. "Yeah, I see businesswomen like her every day."

"She is," he kept his voice even as he rested his hands on his hips. "She's from another vineyard near Florence. She took over the business for her father. We are going to mix a few of our wines and make something new. *A partnership*," he stressed. "She flew in for the meeting and is flying out once the contracts are signed. She's also deeply in love and happily married with two children. We were looking at pictures of them when you so graciously threw my wine in my face."

Her stomach knotted, and her heart clenched. She felt sick. "What?" she whispered, the color draining from her face.

"Tell me one thing, Lina, why in the hell would I tell you the things I told you if I was just going to turn around and go after another woman? Why not just tell you the truth?" He stepped closer to her. "If I wanted to date someone else, I'd do it. I don't need to sneak around behind your back or ask your permission."

She knew he was right and that he was angry. He had every right to be, but she couldn't just let it go. Especially not after his last comment. The comment was intended to put her in her place, to chastise her, but all it did was piss her off. As ugly as it sounds, it made her jealous and distrustful.

Tensing, she stepped away from him. *It will only be a matter of time before he goes after a woman that looks just like the one tonight. A man can't control his nature forever, and a man's nature is to 'slip it in, where you could get it in',* the cruel voice in her head taunted.

"By all means, Gabriel, if you feel the need to date whoever you want, then go right ahead. You are your own man. Don't let me stop you."

"You're not stopping me! I'm stopping me," he yelled. "I want you. I love you," he said. "You're the only one I want. Just you." Muttering a long curse under his breath in Italian, he took a deep breath before speaking again. "All my life, there's only ever been you. The only one I've ever seen, that I've ever wanted. Why can't you see that?" he said, practically pleading with her to see the truth.

Shame burned her eyes, and a harsh tingling sensation tickled the back of her throat as a knot formed. Shaking her head, she tried to swallow past the huge lump in her throat. "Gabriel," she croaked. Clearing her throat, she said, "I'm sorry…Adam—"

"I'm not Adam," he growled, cutting her off. "I'm Gabriel. GA-BRI-EL."

"I know, it's just— It's hard for me to…" To what? Separate the two of them? That wasn't true. Separate the hurt they'd both caused her? Wrong again. Gabriel had never hurt her. Even when they were younger, he'd always treated her like she was special.

"Hard for you to what?" he asked, shifting so barely an inch separated them. Tension radiated off of him. "For you to see that I am not him, that I would never hurt you like he did." His eyebrows were thrust down in a deep frown, lips pinched into a thin line.

"I know," she stammered.

"Do you?" He shook his head. "I thought you did, but now, after tonight, I'm not so sure."

She couldn't blame him. There was no excuse for how she acted tonight. Lilian stood off to the side, eyes wide, letting them have their moment. Why didn't she listen to her when Lilian was trying to pull her back from jumping to conclusions? She never listened. Instead, she let the anger and jealousy over seeing him with another woman, a woman she was sure he had lied to her about, take over. She thought she was over the hurt Adam had caused, that she had closure, but if that was true, would this have happened?

They stared at each other for a long time—the silence pushing them further and further apart. Marlina wanted to say something, wanted to sob and throw herself into his arms, asking for him to forgive her. She wanted to beg him to give her another chance, to apologize until she had no breath left.

Instead, all she did was stand there.

Shaking his head, Gabriel looked back the way they had come before looking back to her. "I know you need time to figure out what's going on in your head, and your heart—time to decide if you can trust me, or if you even want to trust me. I'm not a saint, Marlina, and I'm not going to pretend I am. I've been with a lot of women in my life."

She winced at his words. *Fuck, I could've gone without knowing that.* With her emotions all over the place, it was the last thing she wanted to hear. In the same breath, she supposed she deserved it.

"Those other women didn't mean anything to me, and I didn't pretend like they did, because I'm not a liar. I don't cheat, and I don't lie. I always tell the truth, even if it's hard." Resting his hands low on his hips, he looked down and took a deep breath. "I understand you need time, and I'll give it to you. I'll be here, waiting for you to decide if you can trust me, if you can love me…or not. It's your choice if you want to stay locked in the past with *him*, or if you want to move into the future with *me*." His head still bent, he lifted her gaze to meet his. "Don't make me—don't make us, pay for his mistakes." He looked at her long and hard, so long it felt like they were frozen statues, but then, with those last words, he walked away.

She opened her mouth to call him back but closed her mouth. What would she say? He wasn't wrong, and he had every right to demand she deal with at least some of the baggage she had before entering into a relationship with him. Maybe she wouldn't conquer everything, but the foundation in any relationship was trust. She had to trust him before anything between them could work out. Otherwise, they would crash and burn before they even got off the ground.

Completely mortified by her behavior in the restaurant, coupled with the talk she'd just had with Gabriel, as well as the way she was still allowing Adam to control her life, she buried her face in her hands and cried. She sobbed over the painful thought of losing Gabriel, and the old pain from Adam she was still carrying around.

"Marlina?" Lilian gasped, rushing to her aide. "Are you okay?" Lilian tried to push her hair back to see her face, but Marlina refused to raise her head.

"No," she choked out. Sobbing harder, she leaned against her sister for support. "What the fuck is wrong with me?"

"Oh, honey, nothing. You're just confused and scared." Lilian wrapped her arm around her shoulder and pulled her close. "Come on, let's go home."

Marlina nodded but didn't raise her head.

Gabriel sat in his favorite chair on the veranda outside his house. His veranda faced the small pond that bordered Marlina's grandmother's property. The same pond Marlina spent so much time at as a child, teenager, and now a woman. He was half hoping he'd catch her sitting out there by the light of a golden lantern, if only to catch a glimpse of her. Though, thinking about it, he was glad she wasn't out there. Just knowing she was in pain and seeing her, he wouldn't be able to keep himself away from her. Giving her space and time to think was exactly what he needed to be doing right now, no matter how wrong it felt.

Any man who said Marlina wasn't a passionate woman had never made her angry. When she came charging up to the table at *Il Giardino Nascosto*, he was surprised to see her there, but not nearly as surprised as he was by what happened next. Flinging his wine in his face and shattering it on the stone ground at his feet was so true to her Italian heritage, it shocked the hell out of him. Normally so shy and reserved, it was an outburst he hadn't expected to ever see from her.

A smile crossed his face at the idea of having disagreements with her regularly, and the hot makeup sex that would follow not long after. Amazing, passionate, and perfect for him—that was his Marlina. Even if they argued from time to time, they would always make up and would be blissfully happy together in the end.

Brushing his hand against his chin, he took a sip of the fine, single malt Scotch and wondered what she would do. The thought of her walking away from him, away from the passion they brought out in one another, had his balls aching. What if she decided she couldn't do it?

Marlina thought she knew how he treated women, but she had no idea. All the women he saw before her were looking for the same thing he was: fun. And if they were looking for anything permanent, they weren't looking for it from him. In his entire life, one woman had captured his heart, only one. His entire adult life, he'd never gotten over that one woman. The way he saw it, if the other woman he was with couldn't make him forget about Marlina, then there was no use in trying to make something out of nothing. Until he could forget about Marlina, there was no use in trying to give his heart away, because it didn't belong to him. It never had.

Gabriel was good-looking and charming by nature, traits all the men in his family shared. He knew his family saw him as a playboy with women, and most women who talked to him saw him that way as well. Maybe he did allow himself to come off that way, but he figured the women who did want to have some fun with him wouldn't be looking for it to go any further. That way, there was no risk of hurting anyone.

The only woman he'd ever had feelings for was Marlina. He hadn't know if he was actually in love with her, or if it was just the fond memories of a young boy, but the moment he saw her again, he knew his feeling were true. Sleeping with her only cemented what he already knew—he was completely, absolutely in love with her.

The fire, the jealousy, the lust, the sadness, and even the heartache, he'd felt it all in that instant while they were staring at each other outside in the middle of the street. It unnerved him that someone had such control over his emotions. What unnerved him even more was knowing that if she tried to walk away from him, he'd get down on his knees and beg her to stay with him, to give him a chance. Where was his pride? He didn't have any, it seemed. He would do anything to keep her with him and in his life. Gabriel had never begged for anything, but with her, he do a lot more than beg.

"What's wrong with you?" Lucien asked as he strolled out onto the veranda and sat down next to him.

Turning his head, he looked at his twin. On the outside, they were identical, except for Gabriel's tattoos and panache for jeans and t-shirts. The only time he wore a suit was when someone died. Lucien was different. All the man wore was suits. Seriously, he never took them off. The most casual dress he could be caught in was no suit jacket, tie off, and the sleeves of his white dress shirt rolled up to his elbows.

"Do I have to pick just one thing?" Gabriel asked, returning his attention to the pond in the distance.

"Uh, oh." Lucien whistled, reaching over pouring himself a glass of Scotch into a crystal tumbler. "An answer like that can only mean one thing, a woman."

Gabriel chuckled. "Isn't it always a woman," he grumbled.

"Yes," he agreed, amusement in his tone. "What happened?"

Gabriel shrugged. "Marlina." He waited for his twin to say something, maybe even balk in surprise, but he didn't make a sound. He simply looked at his brother, waiting for him to continue. "You're not surprised?"

"About you and Marlina?" Lucien shook his head. "Why would I be? You've been in love with her since we were kids."

Damn, I didn't know I was that transparent. Then again, they were so close sometimes, they not only knew what the other felt, but they also felt it too. "That's refreshing," Gabriel sighed. If only Marlina could understand it as easily as Lucien. "We slept together," he muttered. "She stayed here with me for two days, and we made love like mad. I took her home this afternoon with plans to meet up after my business meeting," he glanced over at his brother. "Which went fine, despite what took place at *Il Giardino Nascosto*."

"What happened?" Lucien asked, eyeing him curiously.

"Marlina knew I had a meeting, but that I was going to come and get her when I was done. I intended to take her back to my place and pick up where we left off this morning," he paused. He didn't have to work for the rest of the week, and with the weekend free, that gave them six days to explore every inch of each other, fucking all over the house and on every surface, he could find. "I took Abigail to the same restaurant for a more comfortable setting while I explained about our wine and the atmosphere we have here. Marlina walked in with Lilian—"

"Lilian? What was she doing there?" His brother interrupted abruptly.

He frowned. "She was with Marlina."

"Was anyone with them? A man?" he nearly growled.

He rolled his eyes, snorting loud enough for his brother to get the hint. "What? No."

"Good." He cleared his throat. "I mean, Lilian was supposed to be working on the catering she's doing for me this weekend for some clients, and I don't want her to fall behind."

Yeah, he doubted that but wasn't in the mood to give his brother a hard time over it right now. "Whatever." Gabriel shook his head. "That's like five days away, Luc. Lilian is a genius, and I'm sure your clients will be completely impressed with her culinary skills." Shooting back the rest of his Scotch, he huffed. "Now, can we finish talking about me?"

Lucien nodded.

"Anyway, Marlina saw me with Abigail and thought I was on a date with her. She thought I'd lied to her and made up the meeting just so I could see Abigail. And let me tell you, that woman isn't nice when she's pissed off. She threw my wine, expensive red wine, in my face, and shattered the glass at my feet. Completely ruined my Gucci sweater."

Luc chuckled. "You sound angrier about your sweater, than the scene she made in front of Abigail."

"Why wouldn't I be? Abigail completely understood. Said she did the same thing to her husband when they were first dating. She suggested I grovel for whatever I did wrong." His lips twitched, but he tried to push the smile away. "It was my favorite sweater." Giving in, he laughed. "*Maledetto*, the passion in her, the fire," he groaned. "It fires me up and turns me on to no end, even though it pisses me off."

"*Hai capito male*," Luc shook his head. "If that's not love, I don't know what is. So, what happened?"

"She ran out after that. I chased her, of course, and told her that she needed to think about things. That son of a bitch, Adam, hurt her more than she's let on, but she has to figure out how to deal with it. If she doesn't trust me, trust us, and trust our love, then how can our relationship go anywhere?"

"Already thinking about a relationship, that's different for you."

"She's the one for me, my *anima gemelli*." He sighed. "There's no one else."

"Soulmate, though? Don't you think that's being just a little romantic?" Luc asked, pulling a Cuban out of the cigar case Gabriel had next to the Scotch.

He shrugged. "When you know, you know."

"The way you tell it, it's like you've known since we were kids."

"I have." He nodded. "Anyway, I told her she needed to decide if she was going to stay locked in the past with him or move into a future with me.

She doesn't believe me though, so I don't know what she's going to do. I half hoped she would run after me saying there was nothing to think about, that she loved me."

"Of course, you did," Lucien said solemnly. "That's what everyone hopes when they've poured their heart out and have no wish to get hurt. When a woman has been hurt, as Marlina clearly has, it takes time. Give her the time she needs to heal and figure things out. She'll choose you, just be patient, *fratello*. She's just afraid of risking everything and getting hurt again."

"And I'm not?" he growled, snapping his head in his brother's direction. "Do I risk less? I never thought she'd come back into my life. I thought she was gone for good. Now she's back, and I can't just let her leave." He shook his head again. "I can't imagine spending my life without her. I love her. I always have."

Luc said, puffing away on the cigar he lit moments ago. "I wish I had some wise words for you, but I'm only gifted in money matters. What are you going to do?"

What am I going to do? Gabriel wondered. In truth, he didn't know. All he could do was give Marlina time and see what she chose. He just hoped it was him, because if it wasn't, he was going to have to start begging and groveling for her to give them a chance. For her to give REAL LOVE a chance.

TUSCAN HEAT

Chapter 13

Why in movies do they always show some big fight between two people who go their separate ways, but wind up coming back together because they miraculously solve all their problems in the last thirty minutes of the movie? Then they go running back together, problems forgotten the second they look in each other's eyes. Those movies suck. I blame them for their totally unrealistic views of romance and relationships. It's supposed to be that way, because who would watch a movie about a romance like my personal life, a train wreck? No one, that's who. They'd be shaking their heads, trying to figure out just what the fuck was going on in her messed-up brain and why she hadn't gone running back to Gabriel yet.

Two weeks. It'd been two weeks since she'd seen Gabriel. It wasn't that she didn't want to go to him, because she did. Sometimes at night, she stood out on her balcony, staring over in the direction of his house, wanting to show up at his door and tell him what a fool she'd been, but that wouldn't solve anything. She realized her issues would still be there, so they'd repeat the same argument, and it would boil down to one fact: she needed to get her head together. Clearing out all the muck was exactly what she'd been doing.

Most of her thinking had been done with a paintbrush and canvas in her hand. Nonna had let her clean out the small shed behind the house and use it for her studio. Day and night were spent in here those first few days after that night with Gabriel. She thought and cried about a lot of things as she dragged bright colors across the canvas, creating landscapes from here and places she'd never been too. Another of a woman sitting by the pond looking up at the bright star-filled sky with the golden glow of a lantern next to her. Her favorite one she did was of a Gabriel's balcony, complete with the vines growing up the stone and through the black cast iron bars. Light poured out from the room, but the man stood out far enough where it only spilled onto his legs, the rest of his body in silhouette.

The one she was working on now was a self-portrait of sorts. One half of her face was makeup free, her eye sparkling with happiness, cheeks rosy, and her lips pulled into a huge smile, the dimple at the corner of her mouth showing. The other side was skull candy face with tears dripping from her eye. There was no smile on her lips and her eye; you could see the sadness in it. The loneliness, isolation, and disconnectedness. It was the way she felt when she first came here before things blossomed between her and Gabriel. He saw inside her. He changed things inside her, and brought out things she didn't even know were broken to the surface. She appreciated that, after all, if you didn't know something needed to be fixed, then you couldn't work on mending it back together. God, she wanted to mend herself back together for her, for Gabriel, for their future. If they still had one. If he still wanted one with her. She was far from perfect, and things were far from being totally fixed but she was her way. This time apart from him made her realize a lot of things with Mia and Lilian's help, extremely painful at times, and she started to fix those things.

"I don't understand why you just don't go over there, Lina," Lilian said, pulling Marlina out of her thoughts.

"And say what? That I fucked up and acted crazy, but I felt more alive with him in those few days we spent together than I ever have in my whole life? That I've found out a lot about myself these last two weeks and am working on my baggage because I want to be with him in a relationship that isn't full of mistrust because of my past?"

"That actually…sounds good." Lilian nodded, a trail of white smoke drifting from her mouth as she slowly exhaled.

"I can't do that." She sighed heavily, shaking her head. "I can't just bust out with something like that. I have to think up something good. I have so much to apologize for." "Seriously?" Lilian rolled her eyes. "You're over analyzing things."

"Over analyzing? How?" She shot a look at her sister, her eyebrows to her hairline. "I threw his wine in his freaking face because I saw him out with another woman and thought he was lying to me. That is not the actions of a sane woman. It's the actions of a woman who has to work up a good apology if she even has a chance of being forgiven."

Her sister tossed her head back and laughed. "I did tell you not to jump to conclusions," Lilian reminded her. Marlina glared at her. "It's called jealousy, Lina. I'm not saying what you did was right, but you didn't know. You saw him there with a young, drop-dead gorgeous…."

"I never said drop-dead gorgeous," she cut in, correcting her sister and slightly miffed that Lilian had described the woman that way. Even if it was true.

Ignoring Marlina's protest, she continued. "You thought what any woman would think; you just reacted without thinking."

"Yeah, like a fool," she grumbled.

Lil laughed again. "Passion isn't always a good thing."

Throwing a peanut at her sister, Marlina sighed. "I'm glad you find this all so amusing. I don't act like that. I'm calm, rational, and I always think before I act."

"Don't I know it," Lil muttered, shaking her head. "You probably haven't done something you didn't analyze in fifty different ways since you were two."

"So?" she huffed.

"So, you've never been in love. There are no rules to follow. No one to tell you what to do. You have to go it on your own and hope you're taking the right step."

Biting her lip, Marlina thought about what her sister said. "I'm starting to realize a lot of things. Especially after the weekend I spent with Mia."

"Like what?" Lil turned her head, looking at her curiously.

"We didn't talk about what happened the whole time, but I did bring it up. I couldn't believe that I was that jealous over a man I'd been intimate with for only two days. Not exactly enough time to build any kind of emotional attachments."

"What did Mia say?"

"She said it wasn't just two days. Gabriel and I had been connected our whole lives, whether we were in each other's lives or not." She took a deep breath. "When we finally came together, the connection was fast because of our unique situation. She said five years isn't enough time for some people to fall in love, and others five minutes is more than enough." She swallowed hard. "Gabriel was the five minutes. Five, was all it took for me to fall completely head over heels. The timing was wrong once but destiny gave us another chance."

"Is she right?" Lilian asked, eyeing her curiously.

"Yeah." She nodded slowly. "I know you were young but is that how you felt with Justin?" Lilian didn't talk about Becca's dad, so much so, that there was very little Marlina knew about the man.

Lil wrinkled her nose like she just smelled something bad. "We were the perfect 'rage against authority' couple. Him, captain of the football team, and me, a rebel who smoked behind the bleachers during school. I thought I loved him, but we didn't exactly get to feel it out since I ended up prego with Rebekah."

"Yeah, I guess teen pregnancy and pissed off parents would be a romance killer in any relationship," she mumbled. "You know, when Adam told me he wanted a divorce, I just stood there. When he told me he never loved me, I still just stood there. He thought it was because the news was so shocking to me, but that wasn't why I didn't react. It was because I didn't feel anything, nothing. And Gabriel—Gabriel thinks my outburst last night was because I haven't dealt with the pain of our marriage ending." It was ironic, the two men she felt polar opposites about, thought the same thing, but for different reasons. "They're both wrong. I stood there because I didn't feel anything, and I don't feel anything now. I think I thought I should, and because of that perception, it created a whole lot of problems for me."

"Okay, I know this is going to be a strange question—but how can you feel nothing?" Lil asked, genuinely curious. "You were married to the man."

"Married on paper only. We'd been sleeping in separate bedrooms almost from the day we were married. A few years before the divorce bomb, he came home only on the weekends and soon after, not even then. Shit, Lil, I hadn't seen him for three months before he packed his stuff and hit me with divorce papers."

"Why'd you stay with him?" As soon as she asked the question, her hand shot up. "Besides Vivian?"

It wasn't that Lilian couldn't believe their mother was behind it, but what she didn't understand was why Marlina listened. "I don't know why I've let her control my life for so long." And she didn't. The more she thought about it, the more it pissed her off. It was becoming quite clear that her mother didn't give two shits about her happiness.

"It doesn't matter that she was doing it." Lilian stood up, closing her book. "What matters is if you are going to allow her to continue."

"What do you mean 'continue'? I'm here, aren't I," she said.

"And you think Vivian's given up?" Lilian laughed. Opening her mouth to say something, she was soon cut off by a very stern, feminine voice that made them both cringe.

"Now, Lilian, I'm well aware of your distaste for me, but there's no need to poison your sister's mind," Vivian purred, calmly walking over to them, her sky-high black heels clicking on the stones up the walkway. She was dressed in a white power suit, dark sunglasses, and her dark hair was pulled up into a French twist. The only color she wore was bright red lipstick. The outfit was always the same whenever Vivian wanted to exert her authority, and so were the intimidation tactics Marlina knew were coming.

Rising to her feet, she knew her mother would disapprove of her outfit. Wearing an oversized, see-through button-up shirt she had rolled up to the elbows with a white tank underneath, she paired it with her favorite cutoff jean shorts. They were super comfortable, but they also showed off her toned, tanned legs. Something her mother would highly disapprove of. Her feet were bare, and her toes were painted a bright red. Her mother always said red only belonged on a woman's lips, never anywhere else—unless she was a prostitute. What would piss her off the most? The fact that there were streaks of paint across her shirt from her haste to get what was in her head onto the canvas in front of her. Vivian hated her love for painting and thought she had beat it out her years ago.

"Why?" Lilian challenged. "That's why you're here, isn't it? To scold her and fly her back to the States with you. Back to being the perfect cutout daughter, with the perfect cutout marriage. Back to being completely unhappy with a fake life you're so good at portraying."

Vivian's gaze sliced to her other daughter. "Well, since I'm not here to see my biggest disappointment, why don't you leave us alone?"

"Like Hell," Lilian snapped, crossing her arms over her chest. "This is *my* home. I go where I fucking want."

Her mother turned her eyes to Marlina. "Marlina."

Taking a deep breath, Marlina looked at her sister. She hoped to convey with her eyes that she wasn't doing this because their mother commanded her, but because she needed to. Standing up to Vivian was something she needed to do on her own.

"It's okay," Marlina said softly.

Her sister looked like she was about to blow a gasket, but to her credit, she didn't say a word. Lilian glared at their mother, huffed, and walked inside. Marlina knew that if she needed her, she'd come out in a heartbeat.

Turning back to face Vivian, she greeted her coldly. "Mother."

Vivian gave her a disapproving once over. "I see you've gotten comfortable in your brief time here and started the ridiculous hobby of yours, again."

"It's almost summer, and painting is not ridiculous, and it's not a hobby," she defended. Her mother never dressed down, rain or shine. She was always dressed like she was going to a board meeting.

"Whatever." She flicked her hand, frivolously. "Go, gather your things. I've got us a flight booked back to the States at seven. I don't want to stay here any longer than I have to." She turned to walk back the way she'd come, no doubt, a limo waiting for her at the front of the house.

Tightening her hands into a fist, she straightened her spine. "No."

Vivian froze. Marlina could see the heartless steel that made up her mother's spine snap into place. "Excuse me?" she asked, turning her head in Marlina's direction.

Gathering her courage, Marlina pushed her nerves down to her gut. It was hard to stand up to someone who'd been your own personal tyrant most of your life, and that's exactly what Vivian was to her. A tyrant, planning out her life, right down to the smallest detail of the clothing she wore. Of course, she'd picked a husband that wouldn't fight her for control. He wouldn't care because he had no interest in his wife. It was a marriage of convenience with the right connections and growth in status. A business contract. Nothing more, nothing less. Every business contract could be broken, and she was breaking this one. The way her mother achieved her tyranny was by cutting out everyone that was important in Marlina's life. Lilian, Nonna. Her best friend, and Gabriel. Gabriel. Knowing her mother pushed him away on purpose, never let her know about the phone calls or letters, letting Marlina think he forgot about her, all had rage burning in the pit of her gut. Ready to explode through her body like a raging inferno.

"I'm not going with you," she repeated. "I'm staying here."

Facing her again, Vivian had that smile on her face that Marlina hated. The one that looked like she was talking to a willful, spoiled child.

"And I'm going to do what I've always wanted to do, pursue my painting," Marlina said, tilting her chin up in defiance.

Vivian laughed. "I'm sorry, you'll what?"

Keeping hold of her temper, which was not easy, she folded her arms over her chest. "Paint."

"Paint?" Her mother said the word like she couldn't quite understand what Marlina was talking about. "Paint what? Cups, plates, clothes, that kind of thing?"

Marlina pursed her lips. Her mother knew exactly what she was saying. She made fun of Marlina all the time for having such a passion and wanting to follow it. The few times she'd brought it up to her mother, she was met with cynical criticism. "Just painting—you know, like I've always dreamed of doing."

"Dreamed of doing? Since when?" Vivian scoffed.

"Since forever, Mother, and you know it." Giving her mother a small glare, she walked over to the table and poured herself a glass of the Chianti. Breathing deep, she drew the fruity flavor into her lungs and took a sip. It was from Gabriel's vineyard. He gifted it to her, and it was odd, but she felt him in that sip of wine. It felt like he was there with her, giving her the courage to stand up for what she wanted. To stand up for the life she wanted. If she gave into her mother now, not only would she be heading back to the States, but Gabriel would be out of her life for good, and that was so not happening. She wasn't losing him. Not again. She'd do whatever it took to keep him.

Marlina nearly jolted, that realization rocking her to her core. Do whatever it took to keep him. Of course, that was the answer that she'd been seeking in all these days away from him, with all the talks with Lilian and Mia, and there it was. So simple, so to the point, so soul beamingly true. He had her heart, and she had to risk it to get back what she pushed away. She was scared, no terrified, but the prospect of never trying frightened her more.

"Don't be ridiculous," her mother said from behind her. "You're not going to throw everything away, and we both know it. You've worked too hard to get where you are to let some stupid escapade in Italy take it from you."

"It's not stupid here," she snapped, downing the rest of her wine. "And it's not what I worked for. It's what *you* worked for."

"You don't know what you're talking about."

"Yes, I do," she tossed back. "But I wouldn't expect you to care, considering you never listen to me. The apartment, the job, college, the marriage—they were all things *you* wanted. I never wanted them."

"How are you going to explain that to Adam?" Vivian barked. "What, you're just going to tell him you're ready to throw away your whole life, your marriage, for some romp in Italy?"

"This isn't just some fling, mother," she exploded. Wait…how did she know anything about Gabriel? "How do you know about him?"

"Please," she snorted. "You can't throw away all you have for some…*boy*. Why do you think I took you away from here when you were fifteen?"

She'd known. She'd always known. "He was the only reason, wasn't he?"

"What else would it be?" she seethed. "You think I'm a simpleton who doesn't know what's going on in the head of my daughter? Your father had the stupidest notion that we'd let you choose who you'd fall in love with. We had already discussed that if we had daughters, we would choose their path in life. Not the other way around."

"*You* decided?" Tears of anger burned her eyes. She knew her mother was calculating and cold, but even she was surprised by the extent of her manipulation.

"I wasn't about to let you throw your life away on the likes of some boy with who wasn't going anywhere," she spat. "We knew where your life was going, but when push came to shove, your father couldn't stick it out."

The truth of her mother and father's relationship suddenly dawned on her. "That's the real reason you and dad divorced."

"Yes. Your father was never happy in the States or with my idea of where you and your sister's lives should go. He picked up and came back to Italy, and after your sister screwed up her life, he agreed to take her in."

"You left him because he wouldn't let you dictate who we love?" It was too unbelievable, even for a woman like Vivian, but it wasn't. It was true. Every horrible detail was disgustingly true.

"Yes, and I'm not sorry for it. I've always known where I was going. Where *you* were going."

"You mean, where I could take you," she hollered back. "Cause that's all you cared about, isn't it, Mother? That's all you still care about. Isn't it?"

Vivian looked briefly taken aback by her outburst. Regaining her composure, her mouth flattened into a thin line as she pursed her lips. "Of course not. I care about you and your life."

The words sounded hollow to Marlina, and she knew it was because they weren't true. Vivian didn't care about her life, or Lilian. There was only one thing her mother cared about, and it was crystal clear now. She couldn't believe it had taken her so long to figure out what Lilian had known since she was a child.

Tears rolled down her cheeks as a whirlwind of emotions swirled around inside her, creating a vortex of calamity. Gabriel was the first boy she had ever cared about, and she'd been so devastated by him not trying to contact her. Then her mother keeping her busy with too many things to travel back to Italy for a visit that she never even looked at anyone for years. Until Vivian introduced her to Adam.

Adam was funny, charming, rich, and good looking. They had a lot of the same classes and had a lot of the same goals in life. When he showed her, the quiet studyaholic, attention she was flattered. He was so sweet in the beginning. He invited her to study groups, bringing her flowers and other little gifts. It was a wonderful thing for a woman who'd never really been shown attention from men.

Actually, that wasn't entirely true. There was another young man that was interested in her at the time. They shared a couple of coffee study dates, and he'd flirt with her. They kissed, cuddled, went out in groups together. It was fun, until Vivian caught them together once at a coffee shop near NYU. Marlina could still hear the viciousness in her tone when Vivian declared she wasn't to see him anymore. She had no intention of listening, of course, because what woman didn't like to be appreciated by a handsome man. She wasn't sure how she would get around her mother to see him, but she figured she'd find a way. Marlina didn't know what Vivian did, but she never saw that boy again.

Vivian had taken away the only man she'd ever cared about and pushed away another one she was interested in. All in the name of making sure she was with the biggest asshole bastard that walked the face of the Earth. All for what? So, she could be aligned with a powerful family, who had a powerful firm, so Vivian could start making the high society connections she so desperately longed for?

The first time she slept with Adam, he hadn't even stayed the night with her. He made the excuse of having to get up early for some class, and not wanting to wake up her roommate. They had sex nearly every night because, at twenty, men had a chronic hard-on and relieved it any chance they could get, but Adam never once stayed over.

Come to think about it, Adam never took her on an actual date. He never spent the weekend with her, took her to a football game, or a party with his friends. They never went out to the bar, went out to lunch together, or hung out in-between classes. There was a reason no one knew they were together in school; they were never around each other. The relationship was more like a standing booty call. Their marriage was even worse than their non-existent relationship in college. She thought it was a normal relationship. Of course, why wouldn't she? It was all she knew. Adam divorcing her was the best thing that had ever happened to her because it brought her back here. It brought her back to where she was really loved.

Gabriel was so different from Adam. He was kind, attentive, charming, honest, and above all, loyal. She knew that now. The lust and desire in his eyes was for her and only her. Never once did Adam ever look at her like that. The things Gabriel said to her made her feel cherished, adored, and wanted. She never knew what it was like to truly be wanted with such passion and dedication. She could have had it all sooner if it hadn't been for Vivian and her aspirations.

In the distance, the thunder rolled, and the wind blew hard from the east bringing with it dark gray clouds. Taking a deep breath, Marlina drew in the scent of damp earth and moss. Rain was coming. The gloomy storm approaching matched her mood. Hurt, fear, and anger brewed and swirled inside her.

Clenching her hands into fists, her body vibrated as she stared at her mother. No, Vivian. From now on, she would always be Vivian. This was the woman who'd controlled her, kept her sister and father away from her, didn't allow her to come to his funeral, and pushed her into a relationship with a man who never gave a shit about her, all to gain status for herself.

Shaking her head, she brushed her tears away. "Your precious Adam and I divorced."

"He wants you back," her mother said dismissively.

Shocked, her mouth dropped open. "What?"

Vivian nodded. "He and I talked, and he wants you back. Now, go upstairs so we can get you back to the States where you belong, with your husband."

"You're insane," she said, shaking her head incredulously. "I'll never go back to him and, you're lying. Adam is in love, having a baby, cut off from his father, and not giving a shit." She took a deep breath. "I'm not going anywhere with you. This is me following Adam's example and not giving a shit." The first drops of rain made a plopping sound as they landed on the various surfaces surrounding them. Earth-shaking thunder exploded above them, sending a shiver racing through her entire being.

The only person on her mind now was Gabriel. She needed to tell him how sorry she was, how much he loved him, and how miserable she was away from him these last two weeks. She needed to tell him everything. So much time had been wasted in the past. She didn't want to waste another second.

Marlina turned to walk away, but her mother grabbed her arm and jerked her back around to look her in the eyes.

"Don't you walk away from me," Vivian sneered. "You're my daughter, you go where I tell you to go, when I tell you to go."

Narrowing her eyes, she jerked her arm away. "No. I go where I want."

"And you want to stay here, in this shithole?" Vivian sneered.

"For the first time in my life, I'm going to follow my heart."

"You're going with *HIM*," she balked like she couldn't believe Marlina's decision. To be fair, she probably couldn't.

"I love him." Pity for Vivian filled her. For all the venom and crippling lust for power, she'd never know love because she refused to open herself up to it. Marlina knew what love felt like, what it did to you, how crazy it made you, and she loved every single second of it. It was everything and worth risking everything for. "I feel sorry for you, Vivian. Good-bye."

Dashing past her mother, she raced across the yard, not even slowing as her mother screamed for her to come back. Her heart raced, equal amounts of happiness and terror, shooting through her and overloading her system.

She had to find Gabriel.

Chapter 14

The loud crack of thunder broke, as a bright sliver of lightning split the sky, briefly lighting up the darkness. Rain drizzled, and the wind howled gently. The storm was mild, for now, but it was going to get worse as the night went on. Soon, it would be raging with buckets of rain and wind that would be blowing hard enough to sound like it was trying to knock this stone cottage down. He hadn't wanted to go back to his house. Too much of her was there from the days they spent together. Her scent, seeing her pressed up against the wall, panting, lust swimming in her gaze. God, it was torture.

Gabriel stood in front of the window set in a dark oak frame. With both of his hands braced on the marble countertop on either side of the large porcelain sink, he eyed the expensive, dark silver faucet. He had picked it because it complimented the marble countertops beautifully.

He'd had the entire cottage restored from as many of the original stones that he could salvage and created something new, using the old. This cottage meant everything to him because it was the one place, he'd always been able to run to when his father was being a bastard, and his mother was left crying. When he was a child, he swore he'd restore this place the first chance he got. And that was exactly what he did. After his grandmother passed away, he stayed in this old cottage for three days trying to deal with his heartache. He lost his virginity here, and he came here after Marlina was taken away from him that fateful summer.

While rebuilding, he'd upgraded the stove from the original fire to a cast-iron stove that mixed the past and the modern, creating a beautiful piece that was the center of the small open room. In the living room, he had a small dark brown, leather loveseat, an oversized sofa chair that matched the couch with a small dark oak coffee table rested between the two pieces. There was an end table with a lamp resting at the side of the sofa, opposite the fireplace. On the floor was a large, intricately woven, thick, shaggy rug, which helped to take away most of the chill from the dark wood floor.

The light from the fire cast a golden glow throughout the room, causing the south wall he'd constructed of stone, to glow a brilliant gold. He'd chosen the rock because of the ribbons of gold it displayed; he just knew it would look amazing against the firelight.

Doing most of the work himself, it took him some time to restore, but it was time well spent. There was nothing he was prouder of than this old cottage. This had been his safe haven, and it still was.

Lowering his gaze, he stared at the small, black velvet box on the windowsill. A muscle twitched in his cheek from the force of clenching his jaw. Inside was a platinum sapphire engagement ring he had specially designed for Marlina. Mia had suggested a diamond, but he knew his woman; she loved sapphires.

Will you marry me?

He'd repeated the question over and over in his head throughout the last week. He was certain they were getting back together one way or another.

Whether because she came after him or because he got down on his knees and begged her to give him a chance. It was the easiest decision he'd ever made. He knew he wanted to spend his life with her, and no one else.

He'd planned to bring Marlina here and ask her to let him spend the rest of his life with her. He planned everything down to a tee, but for now, those plans were all shot to hell.

He'd expected her to come back to him before now. Maybe he'd overestimated their connection or how much she felt for him. These last two weeks were slowly killing him, but he imagined she was getting along fine without him. It hurt right down to his core to think that, but it could be true. He loved her, and would never wish any pain on her, but was it asking too much for her to be in pain along with him? Was it too much to ask for her to yearn for him the way he yearned for her? To be as lost without him as he was without her.

Tonight was his limit. He knew he said he'd give Marlina time, that he'd wait for her to come to him, but she was taking too long. There was no way he was going to survive another day without knowing if she wanted to be with him or not, if she loved him, and craved him as much as he did her.

He frowned, squinting his eyes in a useless effort to make out the dark figure moving towards the cottage. "Who the hell would be crazy enough to go out in this weather?" he muttered. Then he realized who it was, and his stomach dropped. "She's fucking crazy," he said aloud, through clenched teeth.

Rushing to the door, he yanked it open and ran outside. Not giving a shit about the freezing rain, and it was freezing. He ran around the left side of the house. She reached the back of the house just as he turned the corner. Lunging forward, he grabbed her hand and pulled her behind him toward the door. He didn't get a good look at her, but he didn't give a shit. He'd get a good look at her after they were inside and out of the icy rain. Then he'd demand to know what the hell she was thinking coming out here in this weather.

Throwing the door open, they stumbled inside, the damn wind nearly blowing them over. Gabriel turned, slammed the door shut, and bolted it. Spinning to face Marlina, his heart ached at the sight of her, and his anger dimmed some. Gently, he brushed her dark locks from her cheeks. Ice cold.

Pulling her behind him, he thrust her in front of the fire and started pulling off her clothes. She stood, shivering, not even trying to stop him from getting her naked. Her olive-toned skin was pale and covered with goosebumps. He tried to ignore her rounded hips, firm thighs, and long legs as he peeled her soaked jean-shorts from her body. Tugging her shirt off in one quick yank, he tossed it aside but left her underwear on, not trusting himself to not warm her up with his mouth.

Grabbing the blanket off the back of the sofa chair, he wrapped it around her shoulders. "Are you crazy?" He asked, feeling on edge from being away from her and then from having to focus on undressing her to get her warm, instead of making love to her, which was what he really wanted to do. "Are you trying to get yourself killed?"

"I had to see you," she stammered as her teeth chattered.

Pulling his shirt off, he tossed it on the stone hearth next to the fireplace. Grasping her upper arms, he stepped closer to the fire. "It's too far for you to run here in a storm." Holding her shivering body tightly to his chest, he ran his hands up and down the outside of the blanket where her arms were, trying to create enough friction to warm her up faster. "It's dangerous. You could have been hurt."

Staring up at him, she shook her head. "I know, but I had to see you."

He tried to focus on her face instead of the fire she ignited inside him. "What was so important that you had to give yourself hypothermia?"

"This," she whispered. Rising on her tiptoes, she pressed her lips against his. Gently, her lips fluttered across his, soft and light, sweet.

He sucked in a sharp breath, taken back by the vicious stab of desire slicing through him. Her touch lit him up like a match to gasoline. "Marlina," he rasped, his body hardening with need. "We have to talk."

Smiling, she wrapped her arms around his neck. "I want to be with you. I'm scared, but I'm more afraid of being without you." Taking a deep breath, she pressed her nearly bare breasts against his naked chest. "I don't know much about relationships, Gabriel, and in a lot of ways, this will be my first one. But there's one thing I do know for certain."

Staring into her eyes, he struggled to draw a deep breath. "What's that?" he rasped.

"I need you," she whispered. Pulling his head down to hers, she slid her tongue across his parted lips before pushing past them and into his warm mouth. Pressing herself more firmly against him, she reached behind her. Seconds later, her wet bra was on the floor at their feet. It wasn't much of a barrier between them, but it had still been a barrier.

He groaned at the feel of her silky skin brushing against his, her hard nipples sliding across his abdomen. Their mouths fused, tasting each other hungrily, tongues twisting together in a dance of need. His hard cock throbbed against the zipper of his pants. Thankfully, when he brushed against the cold, wet material of his jeans the throbbing calmed some. With lust raging through his system, everything primitive inside of him urged him to take what was his, and wet jeans seemed to be the perfect solution to getting himself under control. They needed to talk before this went any further.

He was pissed she'd ventured out into this weather, risking getting lost or hurt. Any number of things could've happened. He was grateful she was here, but the thought of her hurt someplace, and no one knowing, gutted him. Wrapping his arms around her, he drew her soft, cold body against his hot one.

"Marlina," he groaned, feeling his control slipping through his fingertips. "Fuck, you feel so good." His dick was already eager to slam her up against any surface and sink deep inside her hot, tight pussy. Raw need clawed through his veins and roared like a beast in his head, effectively reducing him to only one thought pounding through his brain, *fuck her*.

He told himself not to worry about her coming back to him every single day since he walked away from her in the square. *She'd be back because they loved each other, and love conquered all*, he told himself. Now that she was here, all he wanted to do was kiss every single inch of her, stroke her sweet, hot pussy with his mouth, fingers, and his cock. He wanted to leave his mark on every part of her body and her heart, like she did him. Wanted her addicted to him, so she'd never think of leaving him again. Gabriel would never, not for one second, let her forget how much he loved her.

His right hand trailed down her back to cup her firm, round cheek. Holding her tightly against him, he ground against her, increasing the pressure with every rotation of his hips. Marlina whimpered, her fingernails digging into his forearms. That delicate sound nearly snapped what little control he had remaining.

"Marlina," he breathed against the delicate skin of her throat. Nipping at the tender flesh, he began swirling his tongue around, soothing the small hurt. "I can't go slowly," he rasped, slipping his fingers into her thin black panties, giving them one hard yank and dropping them to the floor. Her skin was cool to the touch instead of the freezing cold from moments ago. He was about to warm her up a whole lot more.

"Then don't," she whispered, jumping up and wrapping her legs around his lean hips. "There'll be another time for slow and gentle." Wrapping her arms around his neck, she looked him in the eyes. Her gaze sparkled with a desire so strong it nearly knocked him to his knees. "I want it fast. Hard." She begged, "Please." Leaning forward, she sucked his bottom lip into her mouth before sinking her teeth into his soft flesh. "I need to feel you, now."

A deep growl rumbled from him as the last ounce of control snapped. He was going to take her fast and hard, just like she wanted—like they both wanted.

The deep growl that came from him had her tensing, and she wondered if her words were a mistake. It wasn't that she didn't trust Gabriel, the opposite actually, she trusted him more than any other man she'd ever known. Once, when Adam was intoxicated and in a hurry, he'd hurt her. She was sore for two days after that night. Adam, well, he thought it was amazing.

As if sensing her train of thought, Gabriel leaned in close. "I won't hurt you," he whispered, brushing his thumb across her cheek.

Her fear instantly melted away, as her lips stretched into a small smile. "I trust you," she said, running her hands down his strong back. His muscles were tense, and his body was trembling as he fought to hold himself back. He wanted to make sure she was comfortable, and she loved him even more for it.

His fingers slipped between her legs, going straight for her clit, the circular pressure made her eyes roll back, forcing a moan from her throat. When he took her nub between his fingers, rolling it back and forth, she whimpered. Electric shocks of pleasure shot through her body, all centering where his fingers worked their magic between her thighs.

"Oh, God," she whimpered again, her fingers digging into his shoulders. "Gabriel, that feels so....Ohhh."

"You like that?" he rasped, pushing two fingers into her slick, hot pussy. She was so wet he slid right in. "God, you're so wet," his hoarse voice whispered in her ear.

"*Ohhh*," she moaned louder, as his fingers slid in and out of her. An intense friction built up in her core, her pussy pulsing against his fingers. Her heart raced, and her breathing rushed in and out of her lungs as he worked his fingers inside her faster. "Gabriel," she gasped. "Now, please."

The telltale jingle of his belt followed by the harsh rasp of his zipper sounded moments before he pushed his pants off his lean hips and kicked them to the side. Without a moment's hesitation, his hard cock thrust toward her, all hot, hard, and hungry. He was so fucking big, it was a tight fit, but she loved feeling every single inch of him stretching her so deliciously. After nearly losing him, she needed to feel him deep inside her, needed to feel that pain. She wanted to feel him pounding in and out of her until they were both completely exhausted.

Holding her tightly, he walked across the room and pressed her back against the wooden door. It was cold, and the combination of his hot, hard body in front of her was making her lightheaded. She held on tight as Gabriel pressed up against her entrance as she angled her hips down, eager to take him inside of her.

"Yes," she cried out when he finally sank all the way inside of her in one deep, hard thrust.

"Fuck," he hissed, balls pressed against her ass. His strong fingers dug into her hips as he pulled back before surging forward, rough and hard, just like he'd promised.

"More," she gasped against his shoulder, moments before she sank her teeth into his flesh.

"Look at me," he demanded. Turning her head, her gaze connected with his. Both hands cupped under her ass to lift her higher, as he picked up his pace. The pressure was building quickly. Her lips parted as she scrambled to keep up with the fire he had raging inside of her.

Tightening her legs around his waist, she gripped his hair, keeping her gaze locked with his. "Harder," she begged. "Please, harder. Gabriel!"

"That's right, baby," he groaned. "Scream my name." Pumping his hips faster and harder, her hips thudded against the door behind her.

The sound of damp, naked skin slapping against skin filled the room, turning her on even more. As the pressure built to a breaking point, she knew she was going to come any second. "Oh, God," she whimpered. "Yes….I can feel——Gabriel," she cried out as her orgasm exploded over her.

Her body began convulsing as wave after wave rolled through her. Her pussy gripping Gabriel's hard cock, milking him for every ounce of pleasure. She came hard, her muscles tensing, fluttering as pure ecstasy washed over her.

Slamming into her three more times, his body went rigid. He shouted as his own orgasm washed over him. Pushing in and out of her slowly, Gabriel rode out each tremor, wringing every last ounce of pleasure from their bodies.

Panting and sated, Marlina hung limp in Gabriel's arms, his forehead pressed against her shoulder. She chuckled. "Holy shit." Lifting her head, she smiled at him. "That was amazing."

Gabriel laughed softly as he withdrew from her, gently setting her feet on the floor. "Fuck yeah."

Running her hands up his chest, she circled his neck with her arms. "I love you."

His gaze shot to hers. "You do?"

She nodded. "Yes. I was scared to tell you before."

He rose a brow. "And you're not scared now?"

"I am, but not enough to keep me away from you." She ran her fingers through his sweat dampened dark hair. "I'm more afraid of not taking this chance with you than the possibility of getting hurt."

"I love you." He brushed her hair away from her face. "Wholly and completely. I would never cheat on you. Never give you a reason distrust me or question my loyalty to you. You believe me?"

"Yes," she whispered.

"Good, because I have something for you." Reaching back, he pulled her arms from his neck and walked over to the windowsill. Turning toward her, he hid the box behind his back as he crossed the room back to where she was leaning against the door, still gathering her strength.

Getting down on one knee in front of her, he held up the velvet box and flipped it open.

She gasped, pressing her hands to her mouth. "Oh, Gabriel," she breathed, her eyes blurred with tears as she took in the sight of the beautiful platinum sapphire ring. "It's beautiful. And it's a sapphire."

Gently, he pulled the small ring from the box and held it up to her. "I can't promise that I'll never hurt you, but I can promise I'll always be loyal to you, and that I'll never break your heart. I will always be here, whenever you need me, and I'll always protect you. I swear to try to move heaven and hell if that's what makes you happy. I can't make any promises, except one, if you become my wife, I promise to love you for the rest of my life." He paused. "Marlina, will you marry me?"

Tears streamed down her cheeks as she stared down at him, taking in the beautiful words he spoke to her. A lump rose in her throat. Unable to speak, she nodded.

A big grin broke out across his handsome face. "Is that a yes?"

For a moment, she couldn't form words. She could only nod. This man was her world, everything to her, the love of her life. "Yes," she choked out.

"Yes." Springing to his feet, he took her into his arms and showered kisses all over her face. "Fuck, Marlina, you have no idea how happy you've made me. I have everything I could ever want, right here in my arms." Cupping her face, he stared down into her eyes, his smile fading. "I love you. I've always loved you. My heart belongs to you, and no one else, forever."

"I love you and only you, forever," she whispered. She knew she could put the past behind her because it was those very painful events that brought her back to Italy, brought her back to Gabriel. It had all brought her back to the arms of the man she was meant to be with, and the life, and love she was meant to find.

It's funny how things turned out, and it's strangely odd how a person could outgrow a part of themselves…especially a sad, lonely one. She didn't know what the future held for her and Gabriel, and for the first time in her life, she didn't care.

With Gabriel by her side, as her husband, she was determined they would make it a good one. Their love was real, and she knew it was going to last a lifetime.

TUSCAN HEAT

Please Review

Did you enjoy this book? Did you dislike this book? Either way, please leave a review and let M.A Gonzales know. Not only does she love to hear from those who read her work, good or bad, but reviews help get her work noticed.

Amazon has a ranking system with reviews. Whenever a review is submitted it makes that author, and their work, suggested more for others who might enjoy it.

Thank you very much.

Lilian and Lucian's story in

Hawaiian Fire

Coming Soon!

TUSCAN HEAT

About M.A Gonzales

I love writing books full of erotic heat with fierce, independent, passionate women and the hot alpha males who love them. I get excited about action packed stories full of excitement that shows a couple's journey, whether it be a personal journey and moving on from the past or falling in love surrounded by danger and adventure. Writing about people overcoming impossible odds and fulfilling themselves and their goals is so important to me, it calls to me. It's the same thing I love to see in real life and deeply believe in my heart that we can all accomplish.

Most of the time I focus on stories that have a dangerous sometimes dark theme. Most are a mixture of action & adventure, and steamy, hot romance. Overcoming deep seated issues personally and showing how it effects their relationship is what falling in love is all about. The constant theme in all of my books is sexy, scorching hot romance. I guarantee that my stories will leave you hot and bothered, panting for more.

A loud, tattooed workaholic, I love reading and the ocean speaks to my soul. I'm a wine and chocolate lover, who stares dreamily into sunsets and vows to one day live by the ocean surrounded by animals, the countryside and a big family.

You can visit her, and see all her works, at www.magonzales.net

She's also available on social media. Those links are available on her website.

Made in the USA
Coppell, TX
23 December 2025

66977117R10106